# This was definitely not a dream...

Breasts. Bare breasts. That's the first thing Joe saw as firm thighs squeezed his hips. "Stay still," the woman on top of him quietly ordered.

What did she mean? He *was* still. Oh, well, maybe there was one part of him that wasn't completely obeying....

The balcony doors slid open, but before Joe could see what was going on, the woman was kissing him.

No, she wasn't kissing him—she was devouring him. He groaned against the mattress. This was better than any dream. Forgotten were the strangers on the balcony, the identity of the woman straddling him, the bizarre notion that he didn't have any idea what was happening. All he could think about was the rush of heat to his groin, the taste of the mouth now plundering his....

Then she moved. *Oh, God, she moved.*

Somewhere in the back of Joe's mind he realized the shadows were no longer at the balcony doors. And his dream nymph moved again—only this time, it was away from him. Joe blinked, trying to focus on the gorgeous, naked woman now standing at the foot of his bed.

In a panicked voice, she said, "I need your help."

Dear Reader,

Is there one thing you've always wanted to do, but never dared try? Have you yearned to shrug off your usual nine-to-five clothing and slip into something a little more adventurous...risqué, even? In *Private Investigations,* Ripley Logan does just that by chucking her job as a secretary for a more exciting career as a private investigator. Only, she doesn't anticipate just how very exciting things will get. And sizzling, sinful Joe Pruitt is all too willing to show her....

An ex-jock turned successful businessman, Joe isn't thrilled when he gets pulled into whatever professional mess sexy Miss Logan has gotten herself into. After all, he's willing to go only so far for a good turn in the sack. The problem is that line keeps getting farther and farther away....

We hope you enjoy Ripley and Joe's sexy adventure! We'd love to hear what you think. Write to us at P.O. Box 12271, Toledo, Ohio, 43612, or visit us on the Web at www.toricarrington.com.

Until next time,

Lori & Tony Karayianni
aka Tori Carrington

## Books by Tori Carrington

### HARLEQUIN TEMPTATION
716—CONSTANT CRAVING
740—LICENSE TO THRILL
776—THE P.I. WHO LOVED HER
789—FOR HER EYES ONLY
823—YOU ONLY LOVE ONCE
837—NEVER SAY NEVER AGAIN

### HARLEQUIN BLAZE
15—YOU SEXY THING!

# PRIVATE INVESTIGATIONS
## Tori Carrington

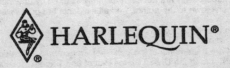

HARLEQUIN®

TORONTO • NEW YORK • LONDON
AMSTERDAM • PARIS • SYDNEY • HAMBURG
STOCKHOLM • ATHENS • TOKYO • MILAN • MADRID
PRAGUE • WARSAW • BUDAPEST • AUCKLAND

This one's for all our online buds at Writerspace.com,
NovelTalk, R.E.A.D., Writers Club Romance Group,
Cata Romance, Compuserve, Romance and Friends,
The Romance Journal and last but definitely not least,
RomEx. Thanks for keeping it real.

ISBN 0-373-25976-X

PRIVATE INVESTIGATIONS

# 1

SLICK FINGERS slid down the length of the long, hard surface then back up again. Moist heat swirled up and around, dampening her skin, making her long for something that was taking far too long to achieve. She gave a good squeeze, gauging the liquid ready to ooze out, then rested her cheek against the familiar object she'd been longing to get her fingers around all day.

Ripley Logan finally judged the bathtub water deep enough, uncapped the bottle of bubble bath in her hand and upended it. She watched, mesmerized, as the contents mixed with the rapidly falling water. She couldn't wait to sink in and soak away the weariness that had built up through the long day.

Okay, she admitted, maybe she'd made more informed decisions in her life. Sitting on the side of the hotel room bathtub, she took a deep breath, allowing the smell of peaches to wash away some of her exhaustion. Who would have thought being a private investigator would be so grueling? Exciting, yes. That was the whole reason she'd learned how to handle a firearm, taken six months worth of specialized classes and studied up on the finer points of surveillance equipment. But her first case, and second day on the job, and she was wondering why no one had told her about the long hours, the countless people who wouldn't talk to her even if she threatened Chinese torture treatment and, well, the plain loneliness of the job. Turning the nearly empty bottle upright, she capped it then stretched to her feet. Muscles she'd forgotten she had hurt. If the reason for her tired state had been interesting, that would be one thing. Pounding the pavement looking for a woman who didn't want to be found was quite another.

She glanced at the time, then took off her watch and laid it on the sink. After midnight, and she was no closer to finding out anything more about a certain missing person, Nicole Bennett, than she had been twelve hours ago, roughly the time her plane set down at Memphis International Airport.

Ripley could practically hear her mother saying, "Maybe they'll take you back at your old job, honey. You do have six years in there. And you're a reliable and skilled worker. I'm sure they'll understand that you've had a change of heart."

Merely imagining the conversation with her mother was enough to snap Ripley's spine straight. The company she'd worked for had been bought out by another company, and a good third of the employees had been offered early retirement or attractive severance packages. She'd been the first in line to take one of the latter. Of course, the part she'd never tell her mother was that she'd seen the offer as a sign that she should stop chomping at the bit and run full out. The perfect opportunity to do something more exciting with her life. Something that didn't involve carrying an extra pair of nylons in her purse and hours shopping for dress shoes that wouldn't kill her.

Not that she expected her mother—or her father either, for that matter—to understand her recent decision. Vivian Logan had been forty-five when she and

Fred had given up trying to have a child of their own and adopted Ripley. They'd always been out of step with her friends' younger parents. While classmates were having cool birthday parties with roller-skating or movie themes, she had suffered through Kool-Aid and cupcake get-togethers with games of pin the tail on the donkey—or worse, piñatas. It wouldn't have been so bad when she was five. But she'd been fifteen.

After the last humiliating experience, when her mother had introduced crazy string to the party and emptied an entire can on top of Jason McCaffee's hand-some blond head, she'd talked her parents into the no-tion that she was an adult and no longer needed par-ties, and her birthdays were marked with a quiet dinner out with her parents.

Yes, she knew her latest career move would worry the hell out of them. But the thought of continuing with her blah life the way it was scared the hell out of *her*. It would be one thing if she actually made her parents happy by leading her life the way she thought they wanted her to. The problem was that they seemed ceaselessly exasperated by her decisions, especially during her very brief but frequent streaks of rebellion that neither began nor ended with adolescence. Rather, Ripley had come to suspect that the alter ego behind those streaks was the real her. And she'd found it was fun finally letting her out to play.

She unstrapped her brand-spanking-new nickel-plated 9mm from her shoulder holster and weighed the two and a half pounds of steel in her hands. Despite how many times she held it, she couldn't get used to seeing herself holding the firearm. She felt like a kid playing cowboys and was ceaselessly filled with the urge to point it and mouth, "Pow, pow!" Only if she did it now, the pow would put a very real hole in something or someone.

The pad of her index finger easily slid to rest against the trigger. Her thumb checked the safety. It was all she could do not to hold it out, close one eye and aim at an imaginary tobacco-chewing cowboy. Instead, she pushed the cartridge release, caught the magazine, then thrust it into place, shivering at the metallic clicks and scratches. She let the powerful firearm drop to her side, then placed it on the sink beside her watch. The way things were going, the only shooting action she'd ever see was at the range. She twisted her lips. Not that she thought she could shoot anyone if the situation called for it. There was a big difference between a black-and-white outline of an individual and an actual flesh-and-blood human being. But just the thought that she could if there was absolutely no other choice made her smile.

And to think, only last week her biggest physical risk had been getting a paper cut.

The problem was that right now she'd be downright ecstatic with a paper cut.

Ripley sighed and pushed her auburn curls from her face. Okay, so today hadn't been as thrilling as she'd hoped. But that didn't mean things wouldn't liven up tomorrow. If foul play was involved in Nicole Bennett's disappearance, then Ripley was going to uncover it. All she needed was a nice long bath and a good night's sleep. Things couldn't possibly look as bad in the morning.

Suds flooded over the side of the tub to pool at her feet. Ripley rushed to shut off the faucet. The water level was midtub. Perfect. She stripped out of her slacks, shirt and panties, then gingerly stepped into the tub. As she stood there, growing accustomed to the heat of the water, she glanced in the bathroom mirror, then did a double take. What was it about hotels that they had to position every mirror so that you had a view of every corner of the place, much less of your personal self? Choosing to ignore the bit of cellulite that begged for exercise on her right thigh, she noted that the bathroom mirror reflected the mirror on the bathroom door that in turn reflected off the mirror in the bedroom, which then revealed a view of the sitting room. She supposed some guests found comfort in seeing their surroundings—and perhaps even their stubborn cellulite. For Ripley it only served as a reminder that she was alone in one of the best hotel suites Memphis had to offer.

She reached out and pushed the door to close it. Only it didn't close all the way. As she sank into the silky bubbles she still had a sliver of a view of the rest of the suite. She closed her eyes, blocking it out.

Bubbles tickled her nose. She wiped them away with a bubble-laden hand. *Well, that worked, didn't it?* She grabbed for a towel and cleaned away the fragrant bubbles, then lay back and relaxed again. Her feet felt as if she'd just run the Boston Marathon. Either that or walked the entire distance between her home city of St. Louis to Memphis. Her body felt like she'd swum the Mississippi, which was visible just beyond the open balcony doors of her bedroom. What she wouldn't give for a thorough massage right now.

As far as she was concerned, massage was a highly underrated skill when it came to choosing members of the opposite sex. Out of the three guys she'd dated in the past five years, a total of zero had known what to do with his hands. She groaned, finding her mood going from bad to worse. After the last dating disaster, she'd given up trying to find that one guy for her, that soul mate magazines touted, the storybook prince little girls dreamed about. She'd gotten to the point where she'd accept companionship. The problem was none of the guys she had dated had been interested in that, either. So she'd decided that her entire life in general needed some livening up. Her friend Nelson Polk had made the fateful mistake of agreeing with her.

"Never found a woman who lived up to my idea of one, you know?" Nelson had said, the steel-wool-like tufts of hair above each ear not stirring as he shook his head and considered his next chess move. The late autumn weather had been mild, the St. Louis park teeming with people out to store up memories to see them through the winter ahead. "Took me three divorces and two bankruptcies to figure that one out. Don't let the same happen to you, Ripley."

That conversation had taken place seven months, two days and ten hours ago. Ripley could pinpoint the exact moment because it had been the only time Nelson had revealed a clue to what had led to his hanging up his P.I. hat and ultimately calling a homeless shelter home and the park his backyard. That moment would be forever locked in her mind because she could envision her life turning out just like his if she didn't do something about it...now.

She had immediately voiced her thoughts to Nelson, expecting objections or arguments or even exasperation. Attempts to talk her out of her silly idea. Instead, he had smiled, neither encouraging her nor discouraging her. And she remembered thinking that if one day she ever did become a mother, that's the type of parent she would be. She wouldn't try to stuff her child into a mold. She would give her son or daughter the freedom to make his or her own decisions.

That conversation had opened an irreparable and irresistible crack in the mold she'd felt suffocated by her entire life, and she'd stepped right through it. She'd looked up shooting ranges in the phone book and held a gun in her hand for the very first time. A life-altering experience. Not because she harbored any secret desire to go around blasting people to kingdom come. That couldn't have been further from her mind. Rather the act of standing there with her feet planted at shoulder width pointing a .22 at the target a mere five yards away shined a spotlight on her and her life. In that one moment she'd known she was solely in charge of the direction she was going. That if she continued going with the flow, making as few waves as possible, she'd end washed up on shore somewhere wondering how in the hell she'd gotten there. She'd been a secretary because... She frowned into the bubbles. It seemed so long ago even she could hardly remember. Her degree was in computer science. But she'd signed up with a temporary agency to get a feel for various companies and ended up staying a secretary.

Going with the flow.

A brief knock sounded on the hotel room door. Ripley snapped open her eyes. Room service forgot something, maybe? The bathroom mirror revealed her chef's salad still on the table in the sitting room, untouched, the requisite glass of water, side order of dressing and bread sticks all there. She reluctantly began sitting up when she heard what sounded suspiciously like a room key being slid into the lock mechanism, then an ominous click she was afraid had allowed entrance.

Someone was coming into her room.

Ripley stared wide-eyed into the mirror even as she slowly sank lower in the tub. The first thing she saw was two hands holding a nasty-looking gun. One that made her 9mm look like a toy.

This didn't make any sense. She'd spent all day beating the bushes, hoping for some sort of revealing reaction to her questions about Nicole Bennett's whereabouts. The most exciting response she'd gotten was a belch from the pawnshop owner whose coffee cup probably hadn't held coffee. At least she thought she hadn't caused any interesting reactions. She'd have to go back over her notes on reading people. Obviously she must have brushed past that section. And now there was one—now two...and three—gunmen slinking into her room.

Speaking of guns...

Sloshing as little as possible, Ripley reached out and grabbed hers from the sink. Then disappeared completely under the bubbles.

Talk about being in over her head....

OH, BOY, was this ever a night to remember.

Joe Pruitt tossed the shoe catalog to the hotel room floor then switched off the bedside light and lay back, folding his hands behind his head. Pale moonlight streamed in from the open balcony doors, reminding him of the overly bright sliver of moon he'd seen earlier. A moon made for lovers, he remembered thinking. He grimaced. Lovers. Yeah, right. For the past ten years his only lover had been his athletic-shoe company, Sole Survivor, Inc. Well, okay, maybe he wasn't being completely honest. There had been Tiffany in Texas. Nanette in North Dakota. Wendy in Washington. He just now realized the correlation between the names and the states, and his grimace deepened. Anyway, his relations with each of the women had lasted no more than a couple of weeks. Long enough for them to figure out that his company came first and everything else a very distant second, and for him to discover that once sex was out of the way, he had very little in common with any of the women. Not that it made much difference. He'd figured out a while ago that settling down wasn't in his blood.

Home base was in Minneapolis, but he had a house in San Francisco, an apartment in Chicago and a condo in New Jersey, and he probably couldn't recite the phone numbers of any of them. His cell phone. Now that was the important number.

Although recently an altogether different number had begun resonating through his brain. The number one. The Three Dog Night song of the same name had been playing right along with it. Where one had been more than okay with him before, now it seemed to be emerging the loneliest number, indeed. He noticed it during his last trip to New Mexico, when he'd landed the big deal with Shoes You Use. Deals like that one always planted a grin on his face. But for some reason, the three months of courting the account, wining and dining the company's reps, then the bigwigs, had felt anticlimactic somehow.

Anticlimactic. Now there was a word. Yeah, well, if he'd paid more attention to the girls at the strip joint earlier, maybe even now he'd be experiencing some real climactic moments. Instead, he'd spent the four hours at the men's club staring at the dancers' feet, fixated on his plans to expand his collection of sports shoes to include daily wear. It was then he knew something was really wrong with him. Here were fantastically sculpted women with perfectly bare breasts, and he was fascinated with their feet.

Joe shifted uncomfortably. He was reasonably sure that the account reps he'd been schmoozing hadn't noticed his distraction. Then again, why should they have? They'd been doing all the things normal men did when a naked woman was shaking her wares in their faces. Namely hooting, hollering and stuffing sweaty bills into barely there bikini bottoms.

Maybe he'd just been to one too many strip joints, he reasoned. There was nothing wrong with him. It was normal to encounter the odd rough patch, wasn't it? Times when things didn't make much sense? When a guy stopped cold in his tracks and asked himself just what it was all about, anyway?

Yeah? Well, then, why had he never experienced one before?

He'd always been happy with his bachelor status. Very happy. A jock of all sports throughout high school, he hadn't allowed his physical capabilities to get in the way of his education and he'd graduated in the top ten percent of his class. An injury while playing college basketball had left him facing a long recovery period. But rather than wallowing in self-pity, he'd traced his injury back to the shoes he'd been wearing and had designed the first of what would be many pairs. He'd graduated, was featured in Forbes at age twenty-five and for all intents and purposes was one of the most successful bachelors on either side of the Mississippi. He'd even finally managed to earn his father's stamp of approval a couple years back when he'd finagled a sponsorship deal with a top player with the Minnesota Timberwolves. A basketball fan from way back, his retired Army colonel father had grinned from the courtside seat the entire season. It was the first time Joe had ever seen tears in his father's eyes, the day when the entire team had posed for a picture with the old man in center court.

Joe found himself grinning. Yes, that had definitely been a highlight. And his actions had earned him an ally against his mother whenever she launched one of her "I want grandchildren" attacks.

Joe figured he'd had it pretty good. An only child. A successful entrepreneur. A relatively problem-free existence.

Then why in hell did he suddenly feel like he was missing the point? That there was something he just wasn't getting?

A shadow fell across his bed from the direction of the open balcony doors. Probably a cloud. He rolled over, away from the balcony, and folded the pillow under his head. He had a full day on tap for tomorrow. Another tour through the target company's inventory warehouse. A look at charts and graphs of how their other products were doing. Another night spent playing the good old boy.

The sheet around his midsection stirred. He grimaced and looked at it. What the hell?

His thoughts stopped completely when a slender female hand circled his waist from behind. Simultaneously, he felt a hot, wet body slide against his back. A very naked, hot, damp body.

Had he fallen asleep? Was this a wet dream, like the ones he used to have when he was seventeen?

The hand rested against his abs between his ribs and his navel. His stomach automatically tightened. The smell of peaches teased his nose. The details seemed very real to him. And if he was asleep, he wanted to get a glimpse of this dream girl.

He moved to turn around.

"No, don't!" a female voice whispered, the arm tightening around his waist, the hand slipping a little lower.

Joe swallowed hard. Definitely not a dream.

Sounds of footsteps on the balcony, and more shadows fell across his bed. Then suddenly, where he'd been pinned in place moments ago, the same arm was flattening him on his back and the woman was straddling him.

Breasts. Bare breasts. That's the first thing Joe saw as firm thighs squeezed his hips. The same type of breasts that hadn't moved him one iota at the strip joint earlier but now made his mouth water, the stiff, peaked tips swaying a mere inch or so away.

The woman bent forward. "Stay still," she quietly ordered.

What did she mean? He *was* still.

Oh. Well, maybe there was one part of him that wasn't completely obeying.

The sound of the balcony doors being slid open, then the woman was kissing him.

No, she wasn't kissing him. She was on the brink of devouring him. The instant her lips pressed against his, her tongue darted shamelessly inside his mouth, along the length of his, then around the interior like it was a hot, dark cave she was determined to map out.

Joe stared at her, bug-eyed in the dim yellow light. Lots of dark curly hair, wide, dark eyes—her tongue dipped again, flicking against his—and a hotly decadent mouth.

He groaned against the mattress and lifted his

hands, burying his fingers in the mass of damp fragrant curls tickling his face.

Sweet Jesus, but this was better than any dream. Forgotten were the strangers on his balcony, the identity of the woman straddling him, the bizarre notion that he didn't have any idea what was happening. All he could think about was the rush of heat to his groin, the *thunk thunk* of his heartbeat in his chest, the taste of the mouth even now plundering his, the feel of soft curls clasped in his fingers.

Then she moved.

Oh, God, she moved.

Joe had to break contact with that incredible mouth and groan as his erection pressed into the V of her thighs. He grasped her bare hips and held her still, his hips jutting upward against her.

Somewhere in the back of his mind, he realized the shadows were no longer at the balcony doors.

The dream nymph on top of him moved again. But this time it was away.

Joe reached for the shadowy silhouette but missed as she padded toward the balcony. A dull click, a rasp of fabric, then the light next to his bedside table was switched on.

Joe blinked at the woman standing in front of the backdrop of the closed balcony doors and heavy maroon curtains, finding her visually every inch as delectable as she had felt. Wild, curly auburn hair framed her oval face, contrasting against her pale skin, the length brushing her shoulders. Breasts full and pouty stood high on her chest, shadowing the slender waist below. The triangle of fleecy curls between her toned thighs was just a shade darker than her hair and seemed to point toward her legs—wondrously long, shapely legs that ended in a pair of sexy feet.

But it was her eyes, almond shaped, brown and large as chestnuts, that told him what had just happened was an aberration.

"I need your help," she said, her voice void of the sexy whisper of moments ago and filled with what he could only equate with panic.

# 2

*WELL, THIS WAS NEW.*

Ripley stared through the peephole in the door. Two of the three gunmen left her room then strode down the hall, obviously minus one of their buddies. Had he stayed behind in her room in case she returned? She jumped when the gruesome twosome seemed to look directly at her before stepping into the elevator. But that was ridiculous—they couldn't see her through the peephole. She drew her head back. Could they?

She turned, her hands flat against the thick metal door. The only problem was that the new view offered another unfamiliar man who also made her want to jump. But for altogether different reasons.

Peering at him through the open door to the bedroom, she saw him lying on his side against the crisp white bed linens, one elbow propping him up, the top sheet draped across his bare waist. Ripley's heart felt like it might beat straight out of her chest. When she'd formulated her plan in her bathtub, she hadn't thought beyond getting out of her hotel room—stat. She lay under cover of the bubbles for as long as she could, avoided a probing with what she thought looked suspiciously like a silencer, but the instant the men left the bathroom and were in the sitting area, she'd hightailed it out of the bath and straight through the open balcony doors. Of course she hadn't stopped to consider that she was as naked as the day she was born or that her room was two floors from the ground. She'd merely clutched her 9mm for dear life, eyed her neighbor's balcony some two feet away and acted.

She swallowed hard. She supposed she should be glad her neighbor wasn't some middle-aged, pudgy salesman. But she wasn't convinced that this guy was better. She stared at the *Playgirl* poster material staring back at her. He had tousled deep blond hair with the slightest of coppery tints, a handsome cowlick over his forehead making him look even more devastating. Blue, blue eyes that tempted every last clichéd comparison to the sea, with a fringe of dark lashes. She knew from visual confirmation as well as touch that he was one hundred percent lean, hard muscle. And he was…long. When she'd straddled him, it had taken a bit of a stretch to reach his mouth, a kiss the best she could do at the time to keep him from reacting as the gunmen appeared at the balcony doors. Well, at least she had prevented him from reacting to *them*. To her…well, he'd been a more than welcoming host.

Ripley realized her breath still came in rapid, shallow gasps and fought to control it. The problem wasn't that the guy was handsome. It was that, despite her predicament, for a minute there she'd actually enjoyed the kiss. Enjoyed it? She'd damn near inhaled him when a simple closed-mouth peck would have done.

In fact it had taken the shock of feeling just how thorough his reaction to her had been through his knit boxers to snap her out of it.

She'd never been so fiendishly unabashed in her life. It didn't matter that three ugly guys toting guns had been the motivation. They didn't explain the genuine hunger that had filled her lying on top of a hot, anonymous guy in a dark hotel room.

"I'm, uh, what I mean is..." She faltered, not quite sure what to say to him now that the immediate danger had passed. She rolled her eyes to stare at the ceiling. *You're a P.I., for God's sake. An independent woman in charge of your own destiny.* She blew out a breath. Yeah, right.

"Thanks," she finally, lamely offered, waving her hand in his general direction.

The rasp of sheets. She blinked to see that he had thrown back the top sheet to reveal the other half of the mattress. "Well, don't you think you should give me a chance to give you something to thank me for?"

Ripley stared at him as if he'd gone insane. Then his suggestive, heat-filled perusal of her person left her mind resonating with one undeniable fact—she was still naked.

"Oh, my God." She slapped one arm across her breasts and her other hand over her...oh, my God. It wasn't that she was overly modest by any means. Her mother had always had to remind her to keep her legs crossed when she wore a skirt, or put her robe on over her pj's. But this definitely didn't fall into the same category. She looked first this way, then the other, visually searching the room for something to put on. Against her better judgment, she stepped into the bedroom. The closet door was ajar.

"Wow, the rear view is just as amazing as the front."

Ripley started, then turned slightly, giving him a side view. Awkwardly positioning her leg so nothing showed, she reached in and grabbed a blue oxford shirt from a hanger, pulling the hanger with it. It took some doing but, with her back still to him, she finally managed to shrug into the soft cotton with what she hoped was a modicum of dignity. At least until she realized that the mirror on the sliding closet door allowed the man behind her a full view of the open front of the shirt. And judging by the grin on his face, he was enjoying every moment of it.

She made a face at him. Just what kind of man didn't blink at a strange, naked woman climbing into his hotel bed in the middle of the night? She shakily buttoned the shirt. Scratch that. She didn't want to know. The truth was, she'd come across one too many just like him. Well, okay, maybe not as drop-dead gorgeous, but externals didn't matter in this case. What did is that he was probably just like every other guy she'd ever dated. "Forget the small talk, babe, and let's get down to business."

Hadn't guys figured out yet that a woman needed more?

Then again, she couldn't blame him. Hey, when a naked woman sneaks into your bed in the middle of the night, what do you do? Kick her out? No. You make the best of the situation, right?

She crossed to the bed, noticing his grin grow wider. She grabbed the sheet and gave it a yank. He moved over to make room for her. She smiled and reached toward his crotch.

"Now that's more like it," he said, patting the spot beside him.

She withdrew her 9mm revolver from under the sheet and weighed it in her hand. She was gratified by the vanishing of all amusement from his face.

"Whoa," he said, holding his hands up almost comically. "You climbed into my bed, remember?"

Ripley smiled and sat on the edge of the mattress.

"Yes. And it's a good thing you're used to such events, isn't it? Or else neither one of us might be here now."

She didn't think she'd ever seen a person move quite so fast. One minute he was in a reclining position, looking like temptation incarnate, the next he was standing next to the bed, clutching the sheet to his chest like he'd been violated. Which, she decided, was how he should have looked when she crawled into bed with him. "Let me get this straight," he said. "You're not a...gift from one of my colleagues."

Ripley's brows moved up on her forehead. She polished the nickel-plated gun with the corner of the sheet. "Do you often get gifts of that nature?"

"Never."

"No, I'm not a gift from one of your colleagues. And I'm not housekeeping looking to make your bed while you're still in it. Or room service, wanting to redefine the meaning of the term." She waved the revolver. "Don't worry, I pushed the wrong button and the clip fell out in the bathtub anyway." She put the handgun on the bedside table closest to her, then leaned across the bed, her hand extended. "Hi. I'm Ripley Logan, P.I."

Oh, how she'd always longed to say that. Some of the patina had worn off during her daylong search for answers, since not one person had seemed impressed by the badge she'd ordered from a magazine. But this guy's reaction made all those blank, unimpressed stares worth it. Even if his expression was probably due more to the gun he kept staring at. While the people she'd encountered all day had gone out of their way to see that she didn't get what she was looking for, this one had wanted to give her everything she was looking for. Er, everything she *wasn't* looking for.

A surprising shiver shimmied along her arms then down her back as she remembered the texture of his tongue against hers and the hot, hair-peppered skin of his chest whispering against her hardened nipples. God, but the guy could kiss. She'd give him that. It had been a good long while since someone had made her toes curl.

She watched him, waiting for him to snap to. Only when he did, she immediately wanted the other guy back. This one...well, the amused glint in his blue eyes warned her to prepare herself. "P.I., huh?"

Just as she thought. She finished buttoning the borrowed shirt, her damp hair falling over her face. "Do you have a name?"

"Uh-huh."

She slid a glance at him. "Are you going to share it with me?"

"Depends," he said, looking to where he still grasped the sheet. He dropped the linen then widened his stance, planting his fists on his hips. For a guy in nothing more than clingy cotton knit boxers he managed to look sexier than all get out.

"On what?"

"On whether or not there's a camera crew ready to spring through the door and tell me this is a practical joke."

"Don't I wish," Ripley said quietly, then added while stabbing a thumb toward the hall, "be my guest."

He stood still for half a heartbeat, then strode to the door in the other room.

Oh, boy. Talk about the back looking just as great as the front. He had a pair of buns a girl could dig her fingers into. And thighs that hinted at an endurance level beyond anything she was used to. He peeked through the peephole then turned, catching the direction of her attention. She quickly looked away and reached toward the bedside table where a wallet lay. She flipped it open. "Joseph Albert Pruitt." She closed the fragrant, faded leather and put it back where she found it. "Nice to meet you, Joseph."

"Joe."

She smiled. Joe. She liked that. Where he could have easily pulled off a name like Fabio, Adonis or Romeo, he had a simple, everyday name. But he was far from your everyday average Joe.

She watched as he took a pair of jeans from a chair and easily stepped into them. She swallowed. Of course he was the type to leave the top button open, revealing where the dark V of hair trailing from his navel disappeared into the waistband.

"So," he said. "The way I see it, we have two options." His suggestive grin should have sent her packing. Instead it made her stomach dip to somewhere in the vicinity of her ankles. "Either we both climb back into that bed...together."

Ripley couldn't believe she found the idea very, very tempting. For crying out loud, she didn't know the guy from...well, from Joe. "And the second option?"

Joe ran his right hand over his tousled hair and shrugged. "You tell me what's going on."

AN HOUR LATER Joe sat across the sitting room table from one very hungry Ripley Logan, P.I., trying not to think that under the shirt she wore, *his* shirt, was nothing but a precious expanse of flawless skin and shadowy crevices. She had one knee pulled up to her chest, leaving him to wonder what the view looked like under the table as she popped another French fry into her mouth and chewed. Part of the deal she'd made with him included ordering up room service. Only after the meal arrived would she tell him what he wanted to hear.

Well, not exactly what he wanted to hear, he amended. If he had it his way, she'd be making those quiet little throaty sounds she was making as she ate, but she'd be making them in the bed in the other room.

"I can't believe how hungry I am," she said, digging into a burger the size of a plate, then licking ketchup from the corner of her mouth. "When I got back to my room earlier I couldn't even think of food. Amazing what a little action can do, huh?"

Joe sat up straighter. He wished she were referring to the type of action he was interested in. The sight of her pink little tongue sweeping her lips just about undid him. "Yes, I suppose running from armed men will do that to a person."

She stopped chewing and blinked at him. Then a twinkle entered her cognac-colored eyes. She was enjoying this, he realized. Not the meal. Not his company. Not what had happened between the two of them in that perfectly good, imperfectly empty bed in the other room. No, she had enjoyed being pursued by gunmen—one of whom could still be camped out in her room, if he bought what she was telling him.

"I guess," she said, waving the burger.

"The funny thing is, I haven't a clue who they are or what they're after, even though I know they have to be involved in this missing persons case I'm working on, but considering all the dead ends I hit today, and I mean not one person would—"

Joe took that as his cue that no further participation

was required by him for the time being and tuned out. The way she was going, he figured he had a good five minutes before she ran out of steam and expected a response from him. He sat back and crossed his arms, enjoying watching her. He'd never seen a woman eat and talk at the same time. His mother would have been absolutely horrified. His father would have probably made one of those sounds of disapproval deep in his military throat. But all Joe could think about was how damn sexy the action was. If she approached food and conversation with such vigor and passion, he could only imagine what she would really be like in bed. Ravenous. Insatiable.

Joe rubbed his chin with his index finger. He didn't quite know what it was about Ripley Logan that captured his attention. Yes, she had Julia Roberts's girl-next-door good looks, but compared to the women at the strip club earlier in the evening, she didn't begin to scream bedroom material. But that's exactly where he wanted to get her—in his bed. Take up right where they'd left off.

The top few buttons of the oxford she filched had been left undone, and as she leaned forward to take a French fry from his untouched plate, the shirt bowed open, revealing more than a healthy stretch of soft skin. He nearly groaned, remembering all too vividly how it had felt to have the rounded flesh of her breasts pressed against his chest.

He started coughing and reached for his water glass only to find she'd already drained it.

"Sorry," she said. She wiped her hand on her napkin, then held out her cola. "I guess I was thirsty, too."

So was he, but he wasn't about to say for what. He

gulped the rest of the cola then held out the glass. She narrowed her eyes and took it back.

Brushing her hands together, she said, still chewing, "So that's it. What I know, you now know."

Joe sat back. Well, that had ended quicker than he'd thought. He'd entirely missed all the cues women usually gave when they were reaching the end of their monologues. Which caught him off guard. "Well, that's...interesting."

"Exciting," she said, and that twinkle entered her eyes, making him wonder all over again what put it there. "At least after the bath part."

"Hmm. The bath."

She laughed, and he had the distinct impression it was at him. "You didn't hear a single word I said, did you?"

His brows rose high on his forehead. Women were usually offended when they figured out he wasn't paying attention. She appeared amused. He scratched his head. Go figure.

"Sure I did. I heard every word," he said, feeling required to make at least the token objection.

She pushed her plate away and rested her elbows on the table, then crossed her arms. "So tell me what I said."

Now this he was used to. All he had to do was choose a few words he'd picked up during the past half hour and he'd convince her he had been listening. "There's the missing person...the bath...the gunmen."

Her full lips quirked. "And?"

"And..." He was surprised at his own laugh. "Okay, you're right, I wasn't listening."

Now why had he gone and admitted it? He'd never done that before.

Ripley waved her hand. "That's okay. I don't think I made much sense even to myself. I probably won't until I figure out who those guys are and what they wanted." She looked to her left, then her right, then leaned forward to peer into the bedroom. "Is it nearly two already?"

She began to get up, and he caught her wrist. "What did you say?"

She blinked at him. "Is it two already?"

He shook his head. "No. The other part."

"What? That I'm going to figure out what those guys wanted?"

Yes, that was it. Now that his mind was functioning at least seminormally, an obvious thought emerged. "Don't you think it would be a good idea if you reported them to the police first?"

"Police? Why would I call the police?"

She glanced at where his hand rested against her slender wrist. He swore he could feel the thrum of her pulse there. He removed his hand. "Oh, I don't know. Call me stupid, but if three armed men were pursuing me, and one was still possibly camping out in my room, the police would be the first people I'd call."

She reached out and grasped his shoulder, bringing her face mere inches from his. He caught a brief whiff of peaches. "Don't worry, Joe. I think I can handle a couple of armed men all by my lonesome. That's part of what being a P.I. is all about."

"Uh-huh," he said slowly. "Has anyone ever told you that you're one scary woman?"

She was insane. It was as simple as that. And if he knew what was good for him, he would be picking up the phone right now and calling the police himself.

She smiled, then turned from him, allowing an

unobstructed view of her from behind. Okay, maybe he'd call in a minute. The shirt she wore was creased at her waist on one side, revealing just a glimpse of a curved cheek. He cleared his throat.

"Besides, what do you think the police would say?" she offered along with the fantastic view. But he'd bet she didn't have a clue what she was doing. "'Do you know who the men were, Miss Logan?' No. 'Do you know why anyone would want to hurt you, Miss Logan?' No. Then they'd flick their little notepads closed and tell me to call them if anything else happens." She waved her right hand, hiking up the shirt even more as she walked away from him. It was all Joe could do not to slump in the chair and groan.

She tossed him a glance over her shoulder. "By the way, you're not married, are you?"

"Married?" He all but croaked the word.

She smiled. "I'll take that as a no. Good. I wouldn't want anyone getting jealous over my staying here."

"Jealous?"

"Yeah, you know. Wives tend to get a little crazy when they find other women staying in their husbands' rooms."

"Yeah, um, crazy." Talk about the pot calling the kettle black. "What do you mean by staying? What— here?"

She frowned. "Why, yes. Where else would I stay so long as one of those mean, nasty men is still in my room?"

Mean? Nasty? Joe scratched his head. Did those words come straight from the P.I. academy?

He didn't get a chance to ask. Ripley waggled her fingers at him, then disappeared into the bedroom, not even the view she'd offered enough to take his mind from the situation at hand. "Good night, Joe. Oh, and thanks again."

She closed the door.

Huh.

Joe sat there for long, silent moments staring at the white enamel of the door, trying to convince himself that what had just happened had, in fact, happened. Had she really locked him out of his own bedroom? He slowly shook his head. This was nuts. In fact, not much of what had happened tonight made much sense. First a naked woman smelling of peaches climbs into his bed buck naked and plants a wet one on him, awakening all sorts of reactions he had just been wondering if he'd grown immune to. Then she virtually takes over his hotel room, wearing his clothes and ordering room service on his tab. Now she'd just told him she was taking over his bed...without him in it.

The same woman who claimed to be a P.I. but struck him as anything but.

Making that phone call to the police was looking more and more appealing.

"Oh, no, you don't."

He got to his feet, made it to the closed bedroom door in five strides and opened it. "I think you and I need to have a..."

His words drifted off along with his thoughts. Lying flat on her back, her mouth slightly open, one certain sexy, mystifying Ripley Logan was fast asleep in the exact spot he'd been lying in when they'd, um, first met. Slowly he neared the bed. Although why he was being quiet he couldn't be sure. He *wanted* to wake her up. Didn't he? He grimaced. Okay, maybe he didn't. Well, not to kick her out of bed, anyway.

The top sheet was bunched around her knees. He

reached for it to pull it up then caught himself. Since when had he developed protective instincts? If she was cold, let her cover her own damn self up. He crossed his arms over his chest and stood stoically for a whole two seconds then sighed and reached for the sheet again. Only something else caught his attention. Namely the soft cotton of her—his—shirt. She must have moved around a bit trying to find a comfortable spot. Her squirming had caused the sheet to come off and the shirt to ride up. The hem brushed her upper thighs, mere inches from the area that had driven him crazy ever since she'd covered it. He could imagine the springy curls just under the soft material. Joe swallowed, the sound loud in the quiet room.

There was something decidedly decadent about standing there like that, watching her without her knowledge. Imagining her slick, swollen flesh just under the soft cotton.

*Get a grip, guy.*

Joe shook his head and turned toward the door to head for the couch in the other room. Suddenly, he stopped. Ripley lay on the far side of the bed. That still left three quarters of the king-size mattress free. He ran a hand through his hair. They were both adults, weren't they? Certainly they were capable of sharing a bed without sex being a factor. There was plenty of room. They wouldn't even have to touch. Unless, of course, they wanted to.

Ripley shifted in her sleep, rolling onto her side and bending her leg at the knee. The movement caused the shirt to pull tight across her shapely little bottom.

Without sex being a factor? Yeah, right.

He left the room and softly closed the door behind him.

# 3

"THIS IS THE CHART showing our fiscal growth over the past three years during our contract with your competitor."

Joe sat in the cramped Shoes Plus conference room with the great view of the Mississippi that no one was looking at, trying like hell to concentrate on what the company sales rep was saying. If only the peaks and valleys on the graph didn't remind him of a certain someone's peaks and valleys, he'd probably be having an easier time of it. Unfortunately, the distractedness he'd noticed yesterday, even before one certifiably insane Ripley Logan had thought about climbing into his bed, was doubly worse today. He pinched the bridge of his nose and glanced at his expensively produced graph showing his projections for the next two years if Shoes Plus decided to contract with his company. But he couldn't seem to summon up the energy to do as he planned, which was to use his graph to cover the one the rep was droning on about.

No, he hadn't gotten much sleep the night before. Call him an idiot, but he hadn't called the police. He hadn't been able to do anything more than lie on that uncomfortable, scratchy couch not even trusting himself to go into the bedroom to get the spare linens from the closet. Instead he'd tossed and turned on the narrow sofa, fallen off the sucker no fewer than two times and spent a perfectly miserable night fantasizing what would have happened had he been able to convince the delectable Miss Logan to finish what she had so skillfully started earlier in the night.

Finally, the sales rep put down his pointer and wrapped up his spiel. Ten sets of eyes turned in Joe's direction in unison. He blinked at them, having completely forgotten where he was.

He discreetly cleared his throat, then smiled. "If you'll excuse me for a minute..."

He pushed from his chair and stepped from the room, closing the door against the open mouths that followed his progress. He pulled out his cell phone and moved toward the farthest corner of the waiting area, nodding at a woman waiting there. He punched a number, asked to be put through to someone, then waited. And waited. He waited for a full eight rings before a decidedly sleepy, infinitely sexy voice answered.

"What are you doing answering the phone?" he asked in a fake chastising voice.

He heard a soft gasp, then sheets rustle. "Who is this?" Ripley finally responded.

"Who do you think it is?" Joe turned away from the woman watching him curiously. "The guy you threw out of his own bed this morning."

"Joe?"

"Unless there's someone else you evicted from their room."

"Where are you?"

He glanced toward the closed door to the conference room. He was supposed to be working. "In a meeting."

A long, protracted yawn. "I didn't even hear you leave."

Which was a wonder, because he'd gone out of his

way to make as much noise as possible two hours ago, slamming doors, opening and closing drawers, after the sounds he'd made showering and getting ready hadn't broken the rhythm of her soft snoring. He'd come out of the bathroom with her smack dab in the same position he'd left her in the night before.

"Isn't sleeping so soundly a job hazard?" he asked. "Especially after what happened last night?"

A pause. "I wasn't in any danger after I got to your room."

"How would you know that?"

"Because...because, well, I have a sixth sense about these things, that's why."

"Ah, something else you learned from the private investigator's handbook?"

A soft laugh. Joe found himself smiling.

"Is there something in particular you wanted, Mr. Pruitt, or did you just call to annoy me?"

Joe realized that there really hadn't been a reason for his call beyond seeing if she was still there. And his relief that she was proved a little off-putting. He thought of the display case on the conference table in the other room and asked if Ripley saw it around the hotel room anywhere. She told him to hang on and he waited while she looked.

He supposed he should tell her that he'd spotted the guy left behind in her room leaving at the same time he did. In fact, he'd shared an elevator with him. But that might mean she'd leave the minute they hung up.

Joe glanced at his watch and called himself a moron. A moment later she was back on the line. "Nope. Nothing of that description around here."

"Damn. I must have left it in the car," he said.

"Is that all?"

He grimaced, drawing a blank for other reasons to keep her on the line. Well, aside from the guy. "Yep. That's it."

"Okay. Well, bye then."

"Yes, bye—wait."

He was afraid she'd hung up, then she sighed and mumbled a distracted, "What?"

"Don't answer the phone again. You, um, never know who might be calling."

"I thought you said you weren't married."

"I didn't say I was a monk."

"Oh. Okay."

Joe disconnected the line, waited a heartbeat, then pressed redial. As expected, Ripley picked up on the first ring.

"I thought I asked you not to pick up the phone."

"Well, then, quit calling me."

Joe disconnected again and chuckled as he headed to the conference room, ready to face the suits in there.

RIPLEY REACHED OVER to replace the receiver on the nightstand, then collapsed against the pillows, smiling. And he thought *she* was weird. What kind of person called to tell her not to answer the phone, then called back and checked to see if she would? She stretched. The kind of guy with a sense of humor, that's what.

She settled her head more comfortably against the pillows. How long had it been since she'd dated someone with a sense of humor? A while. Maybe never, even. At least not a guy with the same wicked, inventive sense of humor Joe had. Of course, she and Joe weren't dating. They'd just slept together. In the same hotel room.

She pushed up to her elbows. A hotel room she should be at least thinking about getting out of.

She caught a glimpse of a note next to the phone and reached over to pluck it up.

"Call the police," was written in large block letters. It was signed, "Joe."

She put the paper down and glanced at the clock then leaped off the bed. Was it really nine-thirty already? She'd meant to get up early and try to follow the third guy when he left her room. Assuming, of course, that he *had* left her room.

She crossed to the wall and pressed her ear against it, although common sense told her one person waiting for another to return probably wouldn't make all that much noise. She sighed then eyed the phone. A person waiting for another probably wouldn't answer the phone in that room, either.

She placed an order for room service to deliver to her room. As soon as she broke the connection, she rushed into the bathroom for a quick shower, only after toweling off realizing she didn't have anything to wear. She stood in the doorway to the bedroom and eyed the drawers. Well, she'd already borrowed the guy's bed. A pair of underwear wouldn't be completely out of line, would it? She put Joe's shirt on, fished a pair of those clingy cotton boxers out of the top drawer, then a pair of socks from the next. Not exactly the epitome of fashion, but it would do. Then she hurried to the door to stand watch for room service, wishing she had thought to have something sent to Joe's room when her stomach growled.

Five minutes later she watched the elevator open and a white uniformed guy roll a cart in the direction of her room. She followed it as far as the peephole would allow, then with the security block securely in place, cracked the door open so she could listen.

A brief, determined knock next door. "Room service."

Ripley smiled. She couldn't help thinking that Nelson Polk would be proud of her little ruse. She resisted the urge to open the door the rest of the way and peek her head out, deciding that wouldn't be very smart. The way her luck was running, the guy would spot her when she was trying to determine if he was still there.

Another knock and a more strident call.

Ripley gave in to temptation and her screaming stomach and opened the door. The room service guy was just beginning to turn away from the door to her room when she waved at him, hurrying down the hall.

"Oh, I'm so sorry! I locked myself out of my room."

He eyed her skeptically. "Ma'am?"

"I'm Ripley Logan. This is my room."

He didn't say anything.

"You don't believe me. Okay. I'll tell you exactly what I ordered then." As she told him, he silently read the order. "Convinced?"

He grimaced while she cautiously eyed the door to her room. Was the guy in there even now, watching her? Attaching a silencer to his gun? She shuddered and stepped a little closer to the wall where she couldn't be seen from the peephole. She'd seen a movie once where someone was shot through the peephole. Even if the logistics didn't make much sense, a little caution never hurt anybody.

The delivery guy called to a maid cleaning a room down the hall. Within minutes she was unlocking the door. Ripley hung back, trying to see beyond the small crack.

"Ma'am?" the delivery guy asked.

"What? Oh, of course."

She swallowed the wad of wool in her throat and tentatively pushed the door open, smiling her nervous thanks to the maid. If the guy was in there, she wanted to be sure she could make a clean run for it. Besides, the room service guy was pretty hefty. He would jump in to protect a damsel in distress, wouldn't he? She eyed him more closely. More likely he'd be running down the hall right after her.

Nothing in the living area.

Ripley tiptoed into the room, craning her neck to make out the bedroom. Remembering the mirrors, she glanced behind her. From the living room, into the bedroom, into the bathroom, she saw no scary shadows. She stepped into the bedroom and closed the balcony doors. Whew. He was gone.

THE WOMAN was an ego booster.

Joe grinned at the conference room full of sales reps and company bigwigs, confident that after a sluggish start, he'd made a successful comeback and had just given one of his strongest finishes ever. Jackpot. This contract was as good as in the bag.

"Gotta tell you, Joe, you had me worried there for a while," VP John Gerard said, pumping Joe's hand after he took down his chart and slid it into its carrying case.

"Don't tell anyone, but I had myself worried there, too."

John chuckled and moved away. Joe straightened to shake hands with the remainder of his colleagues, easily moving from speaker to greeter. His secretary, Gloria Malden, once told him she loved to watch him work. That no one could work a room the way he could. It was a good thing Gloria was fifty and a grand-mother or else he might have thought she was coming on to him. Instead, he'd taken her words as a rare compliment. Lord knew he'd had so few of them growing up. And while he'd like to think he'd grown beyond the shallow desire for praise, he reasoned that it wasn't hurting anyone to acknowledge it when the occasional bit did come his way.

"Dinner tonight, right?" Percy said quietly, leaning closer to him in a conspiratorial way.

Percy had been the biggest tipper at the strip joint last night. Joe was surprised he had money left to slip in any more G-strings.

Joe thought of the sexily provocative Ripley Logan and wondered if she was still in his room and whether or not she'd still be requiring his...services when he finished here. He grimaced. Even if she was and did, he had too much riding on this deal to chuck it all in exchange for some amateur sleuthing with someone who was so wet behind the ears she squeaked.

"Mr. Pruitt?"

Joe told Percy they were on, then glanced toward the door through which most of occupants of the room had already exited. His smile froze on his face when he saw the guy he had shared the elevator with that morning, the one who had chased Ripley from her room and into his bed, standing squarely in the doorway. His body— as wide as it was tall—effectively blocked the exit, and two guys with the exact same build and height stood behind him.

Damn.

RIPLEY REACHED across the table and plucked a straw-berry from the nearly empty service tray in her room, then turned over the picture she was staring at. Dressed in dark blue jeans and a purple T-shirt, she felt much better now that she had regained possession of her room and there were no armed gunmen hiding in the shadows. Her chewing slowed as she eyed the security lock on her door. Of course, it probably wasn't a good idea to stick around too long, lest they figure everything out and make a return appearance.

She brushed her fingers on her jeans then turned the photograph right side up again. The black-and-white shot was of a dark-haired woman of about her age who could have been a double for Angelina Jolie, except that her hairstyle was different. But it wasn't so much the woman in the picture that caused questions. Rather it was the picture itself.

Ripley ran her thumb along the length of the photo. It wasn't on traditional stock paper. Rather it appeared to have been run off a printer. And the grainy quality and downward angle of the shot made it look like something from one of those low-end security cameras. Which really didn't make any sense considering she'd gotten the picture from Nicole Bennett's sister, Clarise.

She glanced over the information again. Nicole Bennett. Twenty-eight years of age. Dark brown hair, gray eyes. No noted employment. She'd been visiting her sister one day when she just up and disappeared with the family silver. The pieces, bearing the recognizable initials ZRD, had popped up at a Memphis pawnshop two days ago.

"She does it all the time," Clarise Bennett had said in response to Ripley's questioning stare. "One Christmas she took antique ornaments from the tree."

No, she hadn't reported the episode to the police.

This was a family matter. And all Clarise was really in-terested in was retrieving her silverware and making sure Nicole was all right.

As to the initials, Clarise had said she'd inherited the set from her maternal grandmother.

Ripley propped her chin on her palm and stared at the photo again. What type of person stole from her own sister to finance a trip to Memphis? Allowing, of course, that that's the reason she'd stolen the items. Was she on drugs? Clarise had assured her she wasn't, but Ripley wasn't convinced. Especially when she'd visited Nicole's apartment in East St. Louis and found that it was little more than a room in a flophouse, a fur-nished room with a sink in the corner that could tech-nically be listed as an apartment but was little more than a closet with running water. She hadn't found anything there to give her a clue about the woman she was looking for.

She reached for another strawberry only to discover they were all gone. As were the eggs Benedict, the two pieces of toast, a side of bacon and an extra large help-ing of hash browns and fruit. She glanced at the front of her jeans and groaned. If she wasn't careful, she would need a whole new wardrobe in a larger size by the time this woman hunt was over.

She reached for the phone to call Clarise and give her a status report. Asking for a better picture of her sister probably wouldn't hurt, either. She consulted the file then dialed the number. A moment later the sound of a recording telling her the number was no longer in ser-vice couldn't have surprised her more. She pressed dis-connect and tried again, only to get the same result.

Well, that didn't make any sense. The number had worked just fine yesterday when she'd called to tell

Clarise she was on her way to Memphis. She tried one more time then finally dropped the phone into its cradle, drumming her fingers against the cold plastic, before putting in a call to her own answering machine. Nothing. Not even a call from her mother reminding her to come for dinner Sunday night.

She hated when there were no messages.

A dull, muffled sound came from the direction of the hall.

Ripley nearly catapulted from the chair and fell on her face, given the way she was sitting with her leg bent under her. But that was nothing compared to the way her heart thunked in her chest. She tiptoed toward the door, her hand resting against her chest as if to keep the rowdy organ still.

She knew she shouldn't have hung around as long as she had. She should have gathered her belongings and hightailed it right out of there the instant she knew the gunmen had left. But no. She'd had to sample the room service tray. And while she was doing that, she thought she might as well review the case file, too. No sense wasting any time.

Right.

Another sound.

Ripley scrambled for the bedroom, hoping she wasn't in for a replay of the night before.

WHAT IN HELL was he getting himself into?

Even as Joe asked himself the question, he knew that whatever it was, it was sure to be a whole hell of a lot more interesting than his life had been of late. He got off the hotel elevator on his floor and strode purposefully toward his room. He'd called there no fewer than four times after Larry, Curly and Moe had left him at Shoes Plus twenty minutes ago. No answer.

Which was essentially what he'd given the three men who had introduced themselves as FBI agents. No answer.

Oh, he'd spoken with them, all right. Only he suspected he hadn't given the responses they had been banking on. Instead, he'd asked them how they'd known where he was. The first guy had said they had gotten his name from the hotel, then put a call into his secretary in Minneapolis.

Great. They probably knew more about him than any of the women he'd dated in the past five years.

No, he'd told them, he didn't know the person in the hotel room next to him. And for good measure asked what the guy was wanted for. Yes, he'd had a female visitor last night. A little Memphis treat from his, um, colleagues. Did he know how to contact her? Well, they might try the Kitty Kat Lounge, but he really couldn't give them any more than her stage name.

After talking around in circles like that for fifteen minutes, Joe had somehow gotten away with not even telling them what that stage name was. If it had come down to it, though, he probably would have made up a name. Like Naughty Nelly or something. Over the past ten years, building his own company, he'd gotten good at staving off disaster. He'd never had to lie, really. He'd merely stretched the truth now and then.

Of course he had lied to the FBI agents. Blatantly. Which meant he'd be in deep doo-doo if they figured that out and caught up with him.

After giving a brief knock on the door, he slid in his card key, then opened the barrier. No sign of Ripley, not that he expected one. The fact that the security block hadn't been on the door was a pretty good indication she wasn't in there. Still, he walked to the bedroom. Either housekeeping had already visited or his surprise visitor was a neat freak. The bed was made. The room service tray from the night before was in the hall. He looked in the bathroom. All the discarded towels sat in a neat pile in the corner.

Neat freak. What kind of woman cleaned up a room at a hotel?

He backtracked to the living area, plucked up the phone and dialed the room next to his, although he'd tried it, along with his number several times earlier. No answer.

Great. The FBI was on his tail for Lord knew what reason. And the woman who was the reason for it had as good as disappeared.

Or at least she wanted to make it appear as though she had.

Joe stalked to the balcony and pulled first the curtains, then the doors open wide. He looked from the left to the right then strode toward what would be Ripley's balcony. He hiked his brows up. There was a good two feet between the railings, and a two-story drop. Had she really climbed over, naked, last night?

The question was, was he ready to climb across, fully clothed, in the light of day?

He gripped the railing and looked over the side. An Olympic-size pool sat in a courtyard surrounded by trees. People milled about, but no one seemed to notice the man staring down at them. All it would have taken was one glance and he'd have scrapped any idea of climbing over. He'd been athletic throughout high school and college. Heights were the only thing that had ever gotten to him.

He gritted his teeth and tried to see into her balcony doors, which wasn't going to work from this vantage point. So much for that idea.

The only way to do something difficult was just to do it.

He gripped the railing tightly and vaulted to the other balcony then stood straight up, brushing his hands together in a show of great pride. Hey, what do you know? It hadn't been half as difficult as he'd thought it would be.

He stepped to the balcony door, expecting to find it locked. Instead, it slid easily open.

Damn. Not a good sign. If Ripley was in there, he highly doubted she'd left the balcony doors unlocked.

The white filmy curtain sheers billowed out and hit him in the face. He yanked them out of the way. The bedroom was just a little too quiet for his liking. Then again, Ripley might have hightailed it out of the hotel altogether the instant after they'd hung up earlier. Maybe she'd gone to the police, as his note to her suggested.

Yeah, right.

He hesitantly stepped inside, not knowing what to expect. At least he was fairly sure The Three Stooges couldn't have beat him to the hotel. Then again, who was to say that there were only the three of them?

He grimaced and looked around the bedroom for any sign that Ripley might still be there.

Well, at least the fact that she wasn't a neat freak was reassuring. Whereas she'd straightened up his room, this place was a mess. In the bathroom he made out discarded clothes on the floor. If he stood staring at the red lacy bikini underwear a little longer than he should have, he wasn't going to admit it. He crossed into the living room where a room service tray sat, not a crumb in sight to indicate what it had held. He stepped to it and smiled. The girl had an appetite, he'd give her that much. He leaned beyond the tray to the table. Papers were strewn across it. He frowned. He was fairly certain they were her papers. But had she left them there the night before, or had she been in the room recently?

He backtracked to the bedroom and stood silently in the doorway, gripping the doorjamb speculatively. The closet door was open, revealing no one was in there. The shower curtain was wide, showing an empty tub. He rubbed his chin, then crossed to the bed. Reaching blindly underneath, he groped around a bit. He heard a gasp at the same time his fingers wrapped around a warm, slender ankle. He gave a good tug, and Ripley Logan lay staring at him as if she expected Jack the Ripper.

He grinned.

RIPLEY KICKED at Joe's shins, muttering every last curse word she'd ever learned, heard or sounded like it fit the occasion. "For God's sake, Pruitt, why didn't you say anything when you came in here? I thought you were one of them."

She got to her feet and stood glaring at him, completely humiliated at having been caught skulking under the hotel room bed. And given his expression, she didn't think he was going to make it any easier on her.

"Don't tell me. Rule number two in the P.I.'s handbook. If you hear an intruder, hide under the bed."

She told him to do something that was physically impossible then strode toward the living area. Yes, this might be her first case. And yes, she was probably making a first-class mess of it. But that didn't mean she had to put up with Joe's wiseass remarks at every misstep.

"Where's your gun?" he asked, following her.

She lifted the lid that had kept her eggs warm and snatched the 9mm. She'd put it there thinking that if she was interrupted during breakfast, it would be close at hand.

Of course, the minute she'd needed it, she'd forgotten it. Out of sight, out of mind, or so the saying went. She took some pride in that the clip was firmly in place. At least this time it had been loaded. She chose to ignore the rest for the time being.

"What are you doing here, anyway?" she asked as she swung around.

"Whoa, there."

Ripley found him standing closer than she thought he would be, and the muzzle of the gun nearly pressed against his solar plexus. He carefully pushed the gun and her hand aside.

"Don't worry. It's on safety," she told him.

"Tell me why that doesn't make me feel any better."

She smiled at him. She'd forgotten how enticingly handsome he was. Her gaze caught on his mouth, and she leisurely licked her lips.

"Ripley?"

"Hmm?"

"Don't look at me that way." She watched a swallow work its way down his throat. "You might not like what happens as a result."

For all intents and purposes last night marked their first kiss. But given the circumstances, Ripley hadn't enjoyed it to the extent she would have normally. Gunmen probably had that effect on a woman. But right here, right now, there was nothing to stop her from thoroughly exploring Joe's smart, sexy mouth. She stepped forward, her gaze firmly on his lips. He caught her by the shoulders.

"Sorry, Ripley. Some men might find a woman with a gun attractive. Me? Frankly, it scares the shit out of me."

She realized she still held the 9mm in her right hand and sighed. "Party pooper."

His grin could have coaxed seedlings into full-grown plants. "You had your chance last night."

"Last night I didn't know you."

"You don't know me all that much better now."

She twisted her lips to rid them of the itching. "Maybe. Maybe not."

He glanced at his watch. "And of course you would pick now to change your mind."

"Of course."

He sighed. "I'm supposed to be in a meeting right now. A very important meeting that could have a very important impact on my company."

"Uh-huh." She could tell by the way his gaze kept drifting to the front of her T-shirt and her mouth that the idea of her kissing him was looking better by the second. She leaned in until their lips were almost touching.

"Which, um, brings me to the reason I'm here," he murmured.

"You mean you didn't come back just to pull me out from under the bed?" But before he could answer, Ripley softly pressed her lips against his.

Joe groaned, his left hand going for her right and the gun. He held it still while his right hand skimmed under the hem of her T-shirt to grasp her breast. She dipped her tongue and tasted his lips. Coffee. Something sweet. A doughnut? She worked her tongue into his mouth. Vanilla. Definitely a doughnut. Bavarian cream.

He quietly cleared his throat, flicking the pad of his thumb over her erect nipple. "What I have in mind takes place on top of the bed, not under it...."

# 4

OH, GOD...

Joe had never considered himself a particularly religious man, but standing there kissing Ripley while holding her gun still with one hand, the fingers of his other stroking her bare breast under her T-shirt was the closest to heaven he'd ever come. A heart-pounding mixture of denial and raw need exploded in his groin until he took the gun out of her hand and put it on the table, then backed up until he plunked down in a chair and she tumbled after him. Much maneuvering ensued, and what he had hoped for happened as Ripley put her legs on either side of the chair and straddled him. Preferable would be if she was minus a pair of jeans, but when her pelvis made solid contact with his he forgot about logistics and delved his tongue deeper into her mouth.

In one smooth move her T-shirt was up and over her head, tousling her auburn hair so it fell wild and curly around her face. He hungrily grasped her breasts in both hands. Not too big, not too small, she fit in his palms perfectly. He fastened his mouth over an engorged nipple and generously laved it with his tongue, reveling in the deep sound she made in her throat and the digging of her fingers into his shoulders. He skimmed his hands around her rib cage to her back, then dove toward her lush bottom, dipping his fingers into the waist of her jeans. She felt so softly decadent, so sinfully sweet. He pressed her more tightly against him, filling his mouth with her flesh and bringing his erection more fully against her.

Ripley thrust her hands into his hair and pulled him back and away from her breasts so she could launch a fresh attack on his mouth. "This...is...so...crazy," she said between kisses.

Joe completely agreed. Crazy was exactly the word he'd use to describe every moment of the twelve hours since she first slipped between his sheets and into his bed.

He ran his fingers up and down the hot silk of her back, then plunged them under her bottom as she pushed his jacket back, and fumbled for the buttons to his shirt.

Joe thought he heard a sound in the hall. Still kissing Ripley, he slanted a gaze toward the door. The security latch was securely in place. But when it came down to it, how much security would it actually provide, especially against those three guys?

All too quickly the reason he'd run out on his lunch meeting with a couple of sales representatives and returned to the hotel to see her came rushing back.

"Ripley," he whispered, trying to tear his mouth from hers.

She made a low sound in her throat as she tugged the tails of his shirt from his slacks.

He caught her hands in his and pulled his head back as far as he could without giving himself whiplash. He nearly cursed at the sheer desire he saw reflected in her brown eyes.

"Ripley, we need to talk."

The instant the words were out, the unmistakable

sound of a card key being inserted into the lock came from the door.

In a flash she was off his lap and diving for the bedroom.

Joe began to follow, nearly colliding with her when she backtracked to retrieve her gun and myriad papers from the table. Her hands shook as she grasped all of it and sought safety.

He wrapped his fingers around hers, pulling her to a stop. Maybe it wasn't such a good idea to run with her, or help her run, not considering what he knew. "Ripley, those guys—the ones from last night—they tracked me down to talk to me this morning."

She blinked at him, apparently not understanding at first, then her eyes widened.

"I don't know what you've gotten yourself into, Ripley, or how deeply you're in it, but they identified themselves as FBI."

The lock mechanism clicked. The hell with grappling between right and wrong. He grasped her by the shoulders and thrust her into the bedroom, closing the door behind him just as he heard the outer door get caught on the security latch.

Christ. Joe closed his eyes and cursed. What were the laws concerning harboring a fugitive?

He glanced at Ripley and the panicked expression on her beautiful face. Aw, hell, who was he kidding? He'd bet his belt and his business that she wasn't any more a fugitive than he was. While half a day wasn't a lot of time in which to get to know someone, he doubted Ripley could even bring herself to jaywalk. The woman had made his bed, for God's sake.

The sound of a body being thrown against the outer door filtered through to them.

Ripley gasped then wriggled from his grasp. He watched, frozen, as she stuffed the gun into her jeans and covered it with her T-shirt, then grabbed a duffel bag from the bed. She stuffed the papers into it. "FBI my behind." She rushed toward the balcony.

Joe followed her, the sweet bottom in question looking damn fine in those close-fitting jeans.

"Ripley, I don't think it's a good idea for you to be going to my room right now. They know about me, remember?"

"How much?" she asked, searching his face.

"What do you mean, how much?"

She stared at him.

"They know I'm your next-door neighbor. No, they don't know you stayed in my room last night, but I think they suspect it. Strongly."

"So who did you say you were with then?"

He cleared his throat. "A stripper."

She surprised him by kissing him full on the mouth. "What was that for?"

"A thank-you. You lied to protect me."

That, he had. And he was beginning to hope he wouldn't live to regret doing so.

He watched her throw her bag over the side of the balcony and had the sinking sensation that he indeed *was* going to live to regret it. He looked over the side with her. Her bag was caught in one of the lower branches of a tree next to the pool. He swallowed hard and took a step back, taking her with him.

"What in the hell are you doing?" he asked in a hushed voice.

She frowned at him. "I'm going to climb down to the ground. What did you think I was going to do?"

"Climb down to the ground."

She wriggled out of his grip. Something she was getting good at. Before he could move she had swung her feet over the railing and was crouching to grab the lower bar of the wrought iron.

Joe closed his eyes and cursed again.

She laughed. "What's the matter, Joe? You're not afraid of heights, are you?"

"No. It's you I'm afraid of."

He gripped the railing and watched her let go and hang from the bottom part. Her feet swayed for several seconds, then she gained a foothold on the railing on the balcony below.

Oh, God...

The irony that those were the same words he'd mentally uttered only a few minutes ago when they started kissing wasn't lost on him. He feverishly rubbed the back of his neck, wondering why he and God were getting so well acquainted all of a sudden, and knowing it was because of the sexy little demon now dropping from the next railing...and straight into the pool.

Joe grinned as she broke the surface of the water, sputtering, and gave her a little wave. Then it hit him—the sound of the door about to give way in the room behind him. And there was Ripley down below pulling herself from the side of the pool. In two seconds flat he and Ripley would be separated for what could possibly be forever.

Then where would she be? Whose bed would she crawl into in the middle of the night? What other imbecile would she shock the hell out of with her recklessness?

Before he could talk himself out of it, he gripped the railing and followed Ripley's lead. When he was on the balcony below, he aimed for the cement patio beside the pool. Too late he figured out that a guy didn't have the most accurate aim when he was shaking clear down to his bones. He landed smack dab in the middle of the pool.

RIPLEY'S NECK snapped back as Joe maneuvered his late-model sedan from the hotel parking lot. Even as she twisted the water from her T-shirt and onto the floor, she glanced around the car, which could have been a twin to the one her parents owned, a four-door Lincoln that had old fogey stamped all over it. Either that or pimp. She gazed at Joe through half-lidded eyes. No. He didn't look like a pimp. Despite the power he seemed to wield over her body, she didn't think he intended to use that same body to make money for himself.

She glanced in the back seat.

"What are those?" she asked, staring at about eight shoe boxes.

"Shoes."

She stared at him. "I meant what are you doing with them?"

He glanced at her. "I'm a sports shoe maker."

"A salesman?"

He crooked his neck as if trying to work out a few kinks. "For the purpose of this trip, yes, I suppose you could say that."

Ripley recalled climbing into his bed the night before and being thankful he wasn't a pudgy salesman. Little did she know. He *was* a salesman. Though, thankfully, not a pudgy one. There wasn't an ounce of fat on Joe's long, lean body. He had the physique of a top-rung baseball player. And a completely decadent one-track mind. Just thinking about his searing kisses, both to her mouth and her breasts, made her hot all over, despite the coolness of the water soaking her clothes.

She slid the 9mm from the waist of her jeans and laid it on the seat beside her, then pawed through her duffel bag, thankful it hadn't landed in the pool along with her. She didn't say anything when Joe took the firearm and put it on the floor under the seat. She pulled out a fresh, dry T-shirt and a pair of khaki shorts. With a quick yank, she peeled the wet material from her torso.

The car swerved, throwing her against the passenger door. "What in the hell are you doing?"

She readied the fresh T-shirt to put on. "What do you mean?"

His eyeballs looked ready to pop straight out of his head as he drew to a stop at a red light. "You're..."

She followed his gaze to her bare breasts, shocked right alongside him. She quickly put on the T-shirt, yanking it down farther than she should have. His hot gaze told her that wasn't much better. She glanced to find her pebbled nipples standing out in clear relief against the soft cotton.

She'd been so preoccupied with their flight, she hadn't thought twice about trading her wet shirt for a dry one, completely oblivious to the fact that they were in a moving vehicle in the middle of the day. She glanced out the side window and found an elderly man grinning at her, gums and all, from a bus stop bench. Oh, boy.

Still, Joe's knee-jerk reaction thrilled her straight to her toes.

She longingly eyed the dry shorts she held, then looked at the heavy, damp denim weighing down her legs.

"Don't even think about it," Joe warned.

She smiled. "What?"

"Changing your shorts in here."

"Why?" She batted her eyelashes at him, something she had never done in her life but that felt strangely natural right now. "You wouldn't want me to catch cold, would you, Joe Pruitt? A cold could lead to a nasty respiratory infection. A nasty respiratory infection can lead to full-blown pneumonia. And you can die from pneumonia."

"We can die if I drive the car into a telephone pole, too."

She shrugged and eased the top button of her jeans open. "You don't have to look."

"I don't have to breathe, either."

She laughed. "You aren't really putting me into the same category as breathing, are you?"

"I'm putting looking at a naked woman into the same category as breathing. They both happen automatically. There's no way I'm going to be able to act like you're not doing anything over there."

"Then I'd suggest you pull the car over," she said, and with one wrenching, skin-chaffing yank, pulled her wet jeans off.

The car swerved again, then screeched to a halt in the parking lot of a small grocer. Ripley wriggled the shorts halfway up her thighs and was about to pull them the rest of the way when Joe beaned her in the head with a cardboard windshield shade he retrieved from the back seat.

"What are you doing?" she asked, rubbing the back of her head.

He was staring at her lap. "Are those my underwear?"

She grinned sheepishly. "Yeah."

He muttered something under his breath, then nearly decapitated her with the shade.

"Would you stop?" she said.

"Somebody has to save you from yourself," he said, spreading the shade so it blocked part of her from outside eyes.

Ripley bristled at his words. While they appeared innocent on the surface, she suspected a much deeper meaning lurked just beneath. Only because she'd spent a lifetime listening to similar words from her parents. "Trust us. We know best, sweetheart," her mother had told her when she'd come home with a battered dirt bike at age fourteen, bought with money she'd made baby-sitting and doing lawn work for neighbors in a ten-block area. Her parents had taken the bike away, promising her they'd reconsider getting her another one when she was a little older. Back then, she'd been slow to realize that "reconsider" basically meant "not in this lifetime."

She hated when people tried to take care of her. Her parents she had to put up with. Joe...

She finished dressing then maneuvered to do the zipper. "No need. I'm done."

"Thank God for small favors."

She ducked as the shade made another pass overhead until it was once again in the back seat.

She squinted at him in the bright midday light streaming through the windows. "Aren't you going to change?"

He backed the car out of the lot, nearly getting rear-ended for his efforts. "I would, but I'm afraid I wouldn't be able to get my pants off."

"Your pants should be easier to get off than mine."

He stared at her as if she weren't only missing the

point, but the entire paragraph. She glanced at the front of his brown trousers and saw immediately what he was talking about. "Oh."

"Oh? Oh?" He whipped the steering wheel around quicker than he needed to and was forced to make a correction. "You nearly get us both killed by playing Sally Striptease and all you have to say is oh?"

She tucked her T-shirt into her shorts, then gathered her wet garments. "I would have thought you'd know how to handle yourself around strippers."

WELL, JUST WHAT in the hell was that supposed to mean?

Joe dragged in a deep breath and slowly let it out, still not entirely convinced Ripley had just did what she had. What was she thinking, stripping down to her skivvies, *his* skivvies, right there in the car? He didn't mind so much that he was around to see. But he could have done without the old geezer nearly smashing his stubble-dotted face against the passenger window to get a better look.

The slow, even breathing exercise wasn't working. He was still as aroused as he'd been two minutes ago. And his mood wasn't improving considering he'd just as good as admitted he'd been angry that someone other than himself had gawked at what he wanted all to himself.

He felt remarkably possessive. As though Ripley was his and his alone to look at. Nude. Naked. Bare as the day she was born. Her rosy nipples pert and puckered in the middle of her swaying breasts.

All this and he hadn't even slept with the woman yet.

Yet? He ran his hand restlessly through his damp

hair, then reached across her lap to the glove compartment where he always kept a clean golf towel. If he had a brain in his head, he wouldn't even consider slipping between Ripley Logan's deliciously toned thighs, much less be so obsessed with the idea that he could barely think of anything else. Including the three beefy FBI agents that not only were hunting for her, but obviously already suspected he was linked to her in some way.

He grimaced. If they'd had any doubts before, they certainly didn't now—not with both their hotel room doors securely bolted from the inside, but no one inside.

He pulled out the golf towel and ran it over his face and hair, then offered it to Ripley. She passed on it, saying she was pretty much dry enough already. He was glad somebody was. He felt like he was sitting in a warm puddle. Or like he *was* a warm puddle...of lust.

She shifted on the seat next to him. Joe was almost afraid to look for fear she'd changed her mind about her choice of clothing and was stripping yet again.

What was with him when it came to her, anyway? For three hours last night he'd been in the company of some of the finest-looking ladies Memphis had to offer and spent the entire time staring at their feet. Meanwhile, Ripley had him so hot and bothered that his wet clothes and the blasted air-conditioning weren't enough to cool him down.

He put the wet towel on the seat next to him then made the mistake of looking in her direction. "I was thinking—"

The words got lost somewhere between his brain and his mouth. Ripley was bending over the seat, doing Lord only knew what in the back, her bottom stuck high in the air. The hem of the shorts was fine when she was sitting, but when she was positioned like that...

Whatever ground Joe had managed to recover in the past few minutes disappeared altogether. He nearly ran off the road again. The blare of a horn behind him made his ears stop ringing but did nothing to put out the fire raging through his bloodstream.

"What are you doing now?" he said between gritted teeth, his fingers gripping the steering wheel so tightly he was afraid he might snap it off its mounting.

Mounting. He shifted uncomfortably then slid another glance at her round, well-shaped bottom.

She glanced at him, that same damn innocent look in her eyes. "I'm spreading out my clothes to dry." She finally turned to sit down, though Joe couldn't really say he was relieved.

He had no idea where he was going, but he figured it was good enough just to be heading away from the hotel. He hadn't spotted anyone tailing him, but that didn't tell him much. He didn't trust his abilities to spot someone if they were following him.

Minutes passed. Joe grew increasingly aware that Ripley hadn't said anything for a while. And he suspected she was staring at him. A glance verified his suspicions.

"What?" he asked, not sure he liked the deep furrow between her dark brows or the contemplative way she considered him.

"What did you mean when you said that someone had to save me from myself?"

He loosened the tie around his neck, then glanced down to find he'd never attended to the buttons she'd undone. He pulled the tie over his head and began shrugging out of his shirt. He started to protest when she reached to help. He didn't think it was such a good idea to have her hands anywhere near him right about now. Her fingers slid down his arms, following his shirtsleeves. After she'd freed the soaked material from his body, he was left with his cotton tank top underneath. He drew in a ragged breath when she began to tug it from the waist of his slacks.

"I asked you a question. Are you going to answer me?" she asked, the backs of her fingers grazing his stomach, robbing him of breath before she stripped the tank top off.

Joe swallowed, catching her hands when she aimed for the zipper to his pants. "Not...a good idea."

She stared at him then shrugged and sat back in her seat, crossing her arms over her chest.

Uh-oh. He got the definite impression he'd upset her.

"I didn't mean anything by it," he said, inexplicably irritated that she was irritated with him.

"I think you did," she disagreed. "I think what you meant is that you think I'm incapable of taking care of myself."

He grimaced. "Well, I have to tell you, Ripley, judging from what I've seen so far, I'm beginning to wonder."

She reached for the revolver on the floor by his feet.

"What are you doing now?"

"Pull over," she said.

He looked between her and the gun. "Not until you tell me what you're going to do."

She gave an exasperated sigh, which, coming from her, was almost humorous. Almost. If she hadn't been checking her gun, it probably would have been laugh material. "I'm going to get out."

She slid the gun into her duffel bag, then raised onto her knees, presumably to collect her clothes from the back seat. Joe caught her leg before she could offer him a primo view of her bottom again. "I don't think that's a good idea." He felt her shiver under his touch and snatched his hand back. "Your getting out, I mean. Of course."

"Well, it's a good thing I didn't ask for your opinion then, isn't it?" she said, bending over.

Joe briefly closed his eyes and said a little prayer, then kept his gaze steadfastly focused out the windshield and on the road beyond until she was sitting again.

"Tell me something, Ripley. What would you do if I let you out? Where would you go?"

She shifted on the seat. "What's it to you?"

He backtracked over what had happened in the past few minutes to change the atmosphere between them. He'd grown up as an only child in a house where the only person who had talked had been him. He'd had all his hopes of pursuing a sports career ripped away from him when he was nineteen. He'd gone on to build his own business from scratch and had done a damn good job of it if he did say so himself. After all that, he considered himself quite proficient at problem solving. But when it came to Ripley he drew a complete blank. "Look, that didn't quite come out the way I intended."

"Oh?" she asked with a raised brow that said something along the lines of, "You could have fooled me, but I'm listening."

He ran his hand through his hair again, then glanced in the rearview mirror to find the red-gold strands sticking straight out at different angles. He finger combed it. "Obviously some things have happened over the past day that have given me the wrong impression about you."

"Obviously."

"I'll be the first to admit, I don't know very much about you. So any impression I have is superficial at best."

She nodded, indicating that he was going to have to find his own way out of this.

He blew out a long breath. "What I propose is this," he said. The road he was on was about to dead end near the Mississippi River. He flicked on the left blinker, deciding to drive around until one or the other of them figured out what in hell they were going to do from there...*if* he talked her into staying in the car. "We go back to square one and start over from scratch."

She narrowed her eyes. "How do you mean?"

He slid his gaze over her, then he offered a grin along with his right hand. "Hi. My name's Joe Pruitt, creator and owner of Sole Survivor, Inc. Nice to meet you."

She stared at his hand, then warily put her hand inside it and gave a brief squeeze. He was astounded by how slender her fingers were, how delicate, but forced himself not to let on to his reaction, reminding himself that she knew how to handle a gun.

Then she smiled, the brightness of it, the guilelessness, hitting him both above and below the belt. "Ripley Logan, private investigator," she said, taking her hand back.

Joe stared unblinkingly at the road. Okay, that was easy enough. But since making her angry had been equally effortless, he figured he'd better watch his step from here on out.

Only now that he wasn't preoccupied with the

source of her anger and his irrational desire to keep her in his car, he questioned both at length.

The FBI was looking for her, for crying out loud. And they were probably now looking for him.

It was impossible to believe that just last night he lay in his hotel room bed alone, wishing something would happen to liven up his life. Had he known this was what lay ahead, he would have thought twice about the careless desire—would have nixed it altogether.

"So, Ripley Logan, private investigator. What did you do before you became a P.I.?"

Her smile disappeared, and she turned her head toward the window, away from him. "I was a secretary."

Joe nearly choked.

She glared at him, then said, "Up until two weeks ago."

"Don't tell me. You just up and quit your job one day and hung out your P.I. shingle."

She made a face. "I knew this wouldn't work."

"What?" he asked, trying not to sound too judgmental. "I'm just trying to make conversation."

"No, what you're doing is making me sound like an idiot."

He grimaced. She fell silent again.

"You didn't ask what I used to do," he said quietly.

She blinked at him.

"Before I got into sports shoe designing."

Wariness entered her eyes, but she apparently decided to humor him. She cleared her throat. "So, Joe Pruitt, what did you do before you became a shoe salesman?"

"I played sports."

Her gaze dropped to his chest. "Nice."

He wasn't sure if she was commenting on his answer

or his chest, so he cleared his throat. "I was working toward signing with the pros when my knee imploded."

Her gaze shifted to his face. "Which sport?"

"Basketball."

She nodded, as if that was what she'd guessed.

He shifted in the seat, wondering why he'd offered that information. Not many women asked about what he'd done before. Ripley hadn't, either. It was that he'd offered it that surprised him.

"I thought I saw a scar last night," she said, reaching out to rest her left hand on his right knee.

Talk about your knee-jerk reactions. She took her hand back, and he tried to laugh off the violent twitch of his leg.

He stretched his neck. Not many commented on that, either. His scar. It ran up the inside of his kneecap, a whopping eight inches long and a quarter inch wide. Even now when he looked at it, he was almost surprised to find it there. The doctors had told him he was lucky to be walking on the knee. Of course that hadn't meant a whole lot to him at the time, not when his entire life had revolved around sports.

"That must have been hard on you," Ripley said quietly. "Having your dreams ripped out from under you like that."

"Yeah, it pretty much sucked."

She sat and quietly contemplated him for a long moment. "It looks like you're doing all right for yourself, though. Not everyone can do that, you know. Recover from such a blow. I have a cousin in St. Louis, twice removed on my mother's side, who got into a car accident the night before final negotiations with the Cardinals. He pretty much exists on welfare, beer and Springsteen. Not a pretty picture."

Joe looked at her, really looked at her, hearing what she was saying and what lay behind her words. "I don't suppose being a secretary was your dream when you were a little girl."

Her smile nearly swallowed her face. "No."

"So was Nancy Drew your heroine?"

She stared blankly at him for a moment, then finally shook her head. "Not exactly. I'm a computer programmer by training." She shifted slightly away from him. "Turn left here."

He got the distinct impression that she wasn't going to offer any more. "Why should I turn here?"

She smiled at him, but her expression was determined. "If you're going to question everything I ask, Joe, then you might as well pull over and let me out now. Because this isn't going to work."

"What? Don't you think I have a right to know where we're going? Or would you like me to put a blindfold on?"

Her eyes darkened as her gaze flicked slowly, suggestively over his face. "That's a thought."

Indeed, it was. Only he didn't want to be behind the wheel of a car when it happened. He'd prefer to be in a bed with his hands tied to the posts and Ripley straddling him.

"We're going to check the pawnshop I went to yesterday. The woman I'm looking for...she sold the guy a couple of items the day before yesterday."

"And you think she'll come back?"

She nodded.

"Why?"

Her gaze snapped up.

"Sorry," he said, raising his hands. "Just please tell me it's not women's intuition."

She smiled. "It's women's intuition."

He groaned.

She laughed. "She told the owner she might return today to sell him a couple more items."

He glared at her.

"Gotcha."

That, she did, indeed. Have him. Right by the short hairs. The problem was, he wasn't in a hurry for her to let them go, no matter how painful the experience was proving to be.

She directed him to turn right at another corner a couple of blocks up. It was an area around Beale Street, not as well kept as the infamous street and in need of some tender loving care it probably wasn't going to get anytime soon. A group of black men on a corner stopped talking and turned to watch them drive by. Ripley told him to slow down on the next block.

"Oh, boy," she muttered.

But before Joe could ask her what was wrong, she was burying her head in the crotch of his slacks.

# 5

"I'D ASK WHAT you're doing down there," Ripley heard Joe say as she burrowed her head into his lap. "But I'm afraid you'll stop doing whatever you have in mind if I do."

Ripley rolled her eyes. "Car at noon. Dark four-door sedan. Anyone look familiar to you?"

She didn't hear anything for a long moment, then Joe's car sped up to what she guessed was the speed limit.

"Damn," Joe said, then repeated the word a couple of times for good measure, his thighs growing tense under her cheek.

Ripley tried to ignore the heat radiating through his damp slacks, and the fact that a certain part of his anatomy was mere millimeters away from her mouth. She swallowed hard. "Is it safe to come up?"

"What?" Joe sounded distracted, then sighed. "Yes. Seeing as the reason you're down there isn't the one I hoped."

Ripley sat up in the passenger seat and smoothed her hair from her face, her heart hiccupping. They were two blocks from the pawnshop. Directly across the street sat a dark sedan not all that dissimilar to Joe's. She watched as one of the World Wrestling Federation wannabes got out of the back of the car, looked both ways, then crossed to the pawnshop. She twisted her lips.

"How in the hell did they beat us here?" Joe asked, though Ripley was pretty sure it was a rhetorical question, since there was no way she could know the answer.

"If you hadn't stopped in the parking lot back there to protect my modesty, they wouldn't have," she said.

He stared at her.

She shrugged. "What? It's the truth. It looks like they just got here, which means they beat us by a couple of minutes."

He grimaced. "Yeah, well, if I hadn't stopped, they would have caught you inside the shop." He rubbed his chin. "Besides, given the reason for my stopping, I probably would have gotten into an accident had I continued on, anyway. Then where would we be?"

Ripley couldn't help but smile. His reaction to her changing in front of him had been humorous, yes, but in some strange way, it had also been touching. It wasn't so much that he was trying to save her honor or something equally chivalrous. No, she suspected that one very stuffy Joe Pruitt had wanted to keep anyone else from gazing at her the same way he apparently enjoyed doing.

She turned to stare out the window. Joe had driven toward the Mississippi. The muddy brown water sparkled in the midday sun as a barge, choked with different-colored containers sluggishly made its way toward the gulf.

She couldn't put her finger on it, but for some reason she seemed to be tuned into the same channel Joe was. She instinctively knew when he was looking at her. And it didn't take a woman more experienced than she was to know what he had in mind when he was looking at her. She seemed aware of him on every level. Knew when he thought she was completely nuts...and when he wanted her so bad it made *her* ache.

She glanced at him. At the way his blond hair lay tousled against his forehead, giving him a sexy, boyish look. His bare chest was broad and toned and made her mouth water with the desire to drag her tongue across his skin for a forbidden taste. Which, of course, was the completely last thing she should be thinking right now.

"Something's going on here I don't know about," she said to herself, reaching for her duffel. She took out the crumpled file and smoothed it against her legs before opening it.

"Where should I go?" Joe asked.

"What do you mean?"

"Well, I can't exactly keep driving without a destination."

She hadn't thought of that.

In fact, it appeared she was incapable of thinking about a lot when she was around Joe. She wondered if that's the way it worked with couples. You had to set aside a part of your brain to devote solely to them—for the consideration of the other person's feelings, thoughts, intentions—leaving you less equipped to do things the way you normally would.

Of course, she and Joe weren't a couple. He was just some poor innocent fool who'd gotten into trouble because of her. That he looked anything but an innocent wasn't his fault.

"I don't know," she said softly.

His jaw tensed at her words.

She closed the file. "Look, Joe, I've already told you

that you don't have to do this. If you want the truth, I don't seem to function all that well around you, anyway."

He glanced at her, a skeptical glint in his blue eyes.

"And I don't want to get you into any more trouble than I already have. Whatever that trouble is." She sighed and squeezed the file against her chest. "I think it would be better for both of us if you just took me back to the hotel and dropped me off. I'll get my rental car and..."

"And?" he prompted.

"And what?"

"What do you do from there?"

She shrugged. "I'll figure something out. In fact, I wouldn't be surprised if the answer came to me the instant you're out of the picture."

His lips twitched upward in the beginnings of a smile.

"What?" she asked, inexplicably irritated all over again.

"So you don't function well when I'm around, huh?"

She looked away and waved her hand. "You...mess with my mental wiring, or something."

"Hmm. Or something."

She shifted until her leg was bent against the seat and she was facing him more fully. "What would you suggest it is?"

"Simple," he said, the smile a stomach-tickling grin. "You want me. Bad."

Her laugh was spontaneous, but a tension resonated through her, making it sound husky and sexy.

He looked in the rearview mirror then changed lanes to go into the city. "I have a suggestion if you'd like to hear it."

"Does it include me naked and a bed?"

"Maybe."

"Then I don't want to hear it."

He gave a mock frown. "Okay, then, it doesn't involve either." He glanced at her. "For now."

The promise in his voice sent shivers skittering all over her. She didn't say anything for a moment. Then she said, "Tell me."

"Well, since we've already established that we're in this together for as long as it takes you to find your missing person—"

"Nicole Bennett."

"Yeah, this Bennett person, I suggest we stop at the next diner and have some lunch."

"And this helps us find Nicole how, exactly?"

"It doesn't. It stops the growling in my stomach." He glanced at her. "And gives me a chance to call my secretary in Minneapolis and have her make reservations for us at another hotel. Under another name. Nothing that can lead the FBI—"

"They're not the FBI."

"Okay, then, those guys to us."

"Then?"

He blinked at her. "Then what?"

"What happens after that?"

His gaze swept over her, dark suggestion in his eyes. "Do you want to hear what I hope will happen or what I think will happen?"

Her nipples tightened against the soft cotton of her T-shirt. "The, um, second."

He shrugged and looked at the road. "You call the shots from there. I'm not sure you know a lot about what you're doing, but I can say I know zip about being a private investigator. So I'll get us the safe place to stay, and you'll tell me how I can help you from there."

"Okay."

"Fine."

"Perfect."

"Do you always have to get in the last word?"

Ripley stared at him, realizing that's exactly what she had been doing. A behavior that used to be completely out of character for her. For as long as she could remember, she had been more likely to nod and acquiesce than risk rocking the boat. It had begun with her parents, whom she had yearned to please, then continued with every other person she met, be it through work or in her personal relationships. It was...liberating, somehow, to feel the competitive fire kindling in her belly, making her want to question and challenge everything, consequences be damned.

She grinned at Joe. "Always."

"HERE."

Joe sat back in the diner booth, staring at the cell phone Ripley held out to him. At her request, they'd chosen a diner near enough to the pawnshop to watch people go in and out and far enough away that if the three stooges returned, they'd be safe. Right after they'd placed their orders, Ripley had told him she had an errand to run and disappeared through the door. He'd thought she was going to go to the pawnshop, but she'd headed in the other direction.

She tried to hand him a scratched and dented wireless phone he wasn't sure he wanted to touch.

"What's this?"

"A cell phone."

"I can see that." He took it, and she slid in the booth

across from him. The waitress popped up with their orders.

"Oh, good. I'm starved," Ripley said, licking her lips as her barbecued beef sandwich and fries were put in front of her. Joe made a face at his bland-looking chicken salad.

"Whose is it?" He waved the cell phone to catch her attention, which was focused on her meal.

She took a bite of her sandwich, her tongue dipping out to lick a dot of sauce from the corner of her mouth. An average, everyday movement that had everything but an average, everyday effect on him. She shrugged. "I don't know. I guess it's mine now."

He ordered himself to stop staring at her.

"I bought it from one of those guys on the corner." She stabbed her thumb over her shoulder. "So it's my guess it's hot."

"Hot. As in stolen?"

She smiled. "Yep. I thought that if our new friends were tracing your calls, this would cause them a little pain."

Pain. Why was Joe getting the feeling he was the only one who was going to be experiencing any pain when this was all over?

"And if they're tapping the phone on the other end?" he asked.

She slowed her chewing then swallowed. "That's the line I'm talking about. What did you think I meant? Your cell phone?" She shook her head. "Just be careful what you say. I bought the phone so they'd have trouble tracking you back to where you are now."

He stared at the receiver then cautiously punched out the number for his office in Minneapolis. Gloria answered on the first ring. If she was concerned or curious about his suggestion that she make hotel arrangements under a different name and have all charges billed to her personal account—for which he promised to reimburse her double—she didn't let on.

It was when he asked her to cancel his afternoon, in fact, cancel everything involved with Shoes Plus, that she went silent.

"Pardon me?" she asked after a few moments.

Joe rubbed his face, his salad not looking all that appealing, while Ripley's meal appeared far more appetizing. Of course, Ripley devouring her BBQ was most enticing of all. "Tell them I came down with a bug."

Ripley wrinkled her nose. "Original."

"Gloria, scratch that. Tell them I have a family emergency and had to return to Minneapolis on the first flight out." A roll of Ripley's eyes. "No, no. Make my apologies and pass on that I fell from the second-floor balcony at my hotel and am on the mend."

That got a smile of approval from Ripley, a smile that made his stomach tighten. He pushed his salad away.

"Joe?" Gloria asked, clearly confused.

"What is it?"

"It's just that, well, in the five years I've worked for you, you've never canceled an appointment."

Joe frowned. Could that possibly be true? What about when he'd come down with the flu last winter? Or when his aunt had died a few months before that? He absently rubbed the back of his neck. He realized that neither occasion had caused him to cancel anything related to work. He'd merely worked around the incidents.

Incidents. Is that what his personal life boiled down to? A series of incidents to work around?

He grimaced and said to Gloria, "Well, then, don't you think it's past time I started?"

A soft laugh filtered over the line. "I think it's long past time. But far be it from me to tell you that."

Joe was surprised at his secretary.

They spoke for a couple more minutes, then he disconnected the line. Ripley held out her hand palm up. Joe placed the hot cell phone into it, wondering how long bacteria could survive on plastic.

"What are you going to do with it now?"

"Throw it out."

Joe stared at her, then his food, and forced himself to pick up his fork. Then he changed his mind and waved the waitress over. "Take this back and give me what she's having."

"You're still going to have to pay for this."

"Big deal." He leaned forward, ignoring the waitress as he considered Ripley. "So tell me about this missing person."

Her chewing slowed, giving him little to concentrate on but her mouth until she finally swallowed. He found himself swallowing right along with her. An empty action that made him feel even more drawn to the woman across from him.

"There's not much to tell, really." She dunked one of her French fries first into BBQ sauce then into ketchup. "Her sister called me the day before yesterday and set up an appointment." She smiled. "I'd just placed my ad in the paper, and she was my first call. Well, technically she was my second, but the first doesn't count because I didn't take the case."

"What was it?"

"A man wanted someone to set up his wife with."

"I'm not following you."

She sighed and waved the French fry. "He suspected she was having an affair...with another woman. He wanted to hire me to play bait. Contingent on his getting a good look at me first, to see if I made the grade."

"You're kidding?"

She popped the French fry into her mouth. "Nope." She wiped her hand on her napkin. "Anyway, the second call was from Clarise, Nicole Bennett's sister. She'd asked to come to my office, but since my office is my apartment until I can afford to rent space, I proposed we meet at her house. She'd said something about her husband not knowing about this, and we settled on a coffee place." She tucked her hair behind her ear. "She gave me a picture, gave me Nicole's most recent address and said that during a recent visit Nicole had stolen a few objects from her."

"What did she steal?"

"Silverware—and jewelry, too, though the silver is all she's sold so far. Yes, I know, I was surprised, too. I mean what kind of world is it when you can't trust your own sister, right? Anyway, she told me that, unfortunately, Nicole has always had sticky fingers and that Clarise wasn't so concerned about the stolen objects, she just wanted to make sure her sister was all right."

The waitress delivered his plate, and Joe rubbed his hands together, then dug in.

"I went to Nicole's apartment, but it really wasn't an apartment at all—more like a nightly or weekly room rental. And it hadn't looked like she had been there long."

"Drugs?"

"That's what I asked. But the sister told me she'd never known Nicole to take drugs. And the people I questioned in the building said she'd been quiet and never looked stoned, so..." She shrugged.

Joe considered her around a mouth full of some of the best-tasting beef he'd had in a long time. Probably because it was the only beef he'd had in a long time. "How did you manage to track her here?" he asked.

"That's what Nelson would call a fluke. He says if you're lucky they happen more often than not, but that you can't count on them."

"Who's Nelson?"

Was it him, or had her cheeks just reddened? "That doesn't matter." She waved his question off. "I did the usual. You know, checked the airport, the train station, the car rental places—she didn't have her own car—and came up with a big fat zero. It wasn't until I was at the airport and accidentally ran into an airline attendant not averse to a little cash falling into her hand that I hit pay dirt." Her smile was brilliant. "She recognized a picture I have of Nicole and told me she sold her a ticket to Memphis and personally saw her get on the plane for here the night before.

"So I came here, found the hotel she was staying at and checked into the same room she'd vacated—though I didn't find anything useful in it. Either house-keeping had already cleared all clues, or more likely, given the clean state of the room in St. Louis, Nicole had cleared it herself. Then I started pounding the pavement. The pawnshop—" she jabbed her thumb in that direction "—was my third stop when I got into town."

Joe watched as a taxi pulled up in front of the pawn-shop in question. A dark-haired woman got out, paid the driver through the front window, then walked toward the establishment, a brown bag in her right hand.

"You got a picture of the woman?" he asked.

Ripley nodded, then fished a copy out of the file lying next to her on the table.

Joe glanced at it, then the woman walking into the pawnshop. "Don't look now, but your girl just arrived."

*THIS IS BETTER THAN SEX.*

Ripley's mind paused as she raced through the diner door, her heart beating a million miles a minute. Well, okay, maybe it was just as good as sex, at least the type she was used to having. But she couldn't really think about that now because she was busy closing in on her first missing person.

She should have signed up for this a long time ago, she thought, even if she couldn't quite bring herself to believe her luck. Could Joe have been mistaken? Could the woman going into the pawnshop have just looked like Nicole Bennett? After all, a good hundred feet separated the diner from the shop. Maybe he hadn't gotten a good look.

Or...

Or else he was toying with her. She'd bolted from the table so quickly, she hadn't stopped to consider that option. She glanced behind her to find Joe being tackled by the waitress, likely to pay their bill, and was relieved. She'd have gone into murder mode had she found him still sitting in the booth grinning at her.

The sound of her feet against the pavement. The feel of her hair flying behind her. The burning of her lungs, which revealed how little exercise she usually got. All of it combined to make her feel...well, pretty damn good.

Near the pawnshop, she slowed, her hand clutching

her side. She really needed to get into shape. As inconspicuously as possible, she poked her head around and peered through the grimy glass, then pulled back. She smiled so wide, her face hurt. Definitely one very wily, sticky-fingered Nicole Bennett.

She'd been given strict instructions on what she was to do when she tracked down Nicole. Namely follow her to find out where she was staying, then contact her sister in St. Louis.

She frowned. But the last time she'd tried calling Nicole's sister, she'd received a recording telling her the line had been disconnected.

She briefly closed her eyes. So what did she do?

The clang of a cowbell found her springing from the side of the building next door. She stared as Nicole Bennett came out of the pawnshop, minus one shopping bag and tucking money into the pocket of her jacket.

"Freeze," Ripley said.

Freeze? Had she really just yelled freeze? Good Lord, she wasn't a cop. She wasn't even supposed to approach Nicole. Nicole wasn't even supposed to know Ripley was following her.

Her first case, and she'd already royally messed it up.

Nicole's gray eyes widened in surprise. Then she looked at Ripley's hands, which were obviously minus a weapon, and took off running in the opposite direction.

Ripley took off after her. She didn't know what she was going to do once she caught up with her, but she was trusting she'd figure that one out when the time came.

"Is that her?"

Joe's voice so close to her ear made Ripley scream. Then, before she could stop herself, she lost her running rhythm and started a headlong dive for the hard pavement. The only thing that stopped her from getting pavement burn was Joe's fast thinking. He grabbed the back of her T-shirt, holding her suspended in midair. Ripley jerked her head up, watching as Nicole darted around the corner and out of sight.

She awkwardly regained her footing, straightened her T-shirt, then stomped squarely on Joe's foot. His resulting *yeow* only dented her disappointment.

"What was that for?" he asked, hopping on one foot.

"For making me lose my first missing person."

The only problem was that the person she was working for to find a missing person had also recently joined ranks with those already on the missing persons list. Which left her exactly...where?

She glanced in the direction Nicole went, stepped that way, then stopped and started walking toward the diner. Only the instant she did, she spotted the dark sedan carrying the three bozos claiming to be with the FBI.

Oh, boy.

# 6

RIPLEY KNOCKED briefly on the hotel room door, then reminded herself to stand squarely in front of the peephole. A moment later the door opened, and she stood staring at Joe, who was freshly showered, a towel slung low on his slender hips, his abs standing out in glorious relief. God, but he was magnificent. A true thing of beauty in all the confusion swirling around her.

"Are you coming in or what?" he asked quietly, gripping her wrist then tugging her inside. He looked both ways down the hall, then closed the door.

Ripley grimaced at him, hating that he could stop her dead in her tracks with very little effort. Actually, with no effort. He hadn't done anything but stand there looking like dessert, and her brain completely zonked. All she'd been able to do was stand there gaping at him.

She strode across the room to the king-size bed and flopped down on it, letting her duffel fall to the floor at her feet. Feet that ached from all the running she'd done in the past half hour—first after Nicole Bennett, then from the three goons hot on her trail for God only knew what reason.

Thankfully, she had seen them before they saw her, giving her a good head start. And she'd taken complete advantage of it, ducking inside the antique shop next to the pawnshop and taking Joe with her. They'd pretended to be out-of-town browsers interested in the splotches of red and black paint that somebody called art, waiting until the three men sitting in the car moved on.

After fifteen minutes they had. Then Joe had driven them to the hotel that would be their new digs. She'd insisted on getting out of the car at the corner so they wouldn't be seen together any more than they had to be, gave him a chance to check in and get to the room, then called him using the hot cell phone she bought from the guys on the street corner. Joe told her what room number, and here she was.

She rubbed the skin between her brows, feeling the beginnings of a whopper of a headache coming on. "Are you sure no one can connect your name to the one on the room?"

"Completely."

She blinked at him. He grinned.

"You probably don't want to hear this now, but you could probably run better if you had the right pair of shoes."

Ripley rolled her eyes to stare at the ceiling. "Oh, great, now he's trying to sell me shoes."

He shrugged. "It's what I do. So shoot me."

"Don't tempt me," she muttered under her breath.

Actually, she was more in a mind to shoot herself. *Freeze.* She cringed, still unable to believe she'd yelled that when she'd spotted Nicole outside the pawnshop. The incident played out in her mind like every apprehension scene she'd seen in every television cop show she'd ever seen a rerun of. Who did she think she was, Police Woman? Or worse, Wonder Woman, with her invisible plane and golden lasso? While she was on the topic, why had Wonder Woman carried a lasso, anyway? Anyone who could pull off and pilot an invisible plane certainly deserved a weapon more potent than a wimpy lasso. She couldn't remember why, and that irked her more.

She flopped on the bed and groaned. Here she had probably just blown her first case, and she was thinking about a woman who wore a red-white-and-blue bustier.

Maybe her mother was right. Maybe they would still take her back at her old job. If she offered them the money from the employee package she'd taken and crawled to them on hands and knees, maybe they'd hire her back, no questions asked. Of course, she supposed it didn't help that she'd already spent the money in question, and that she'd said a few unkind words to her immediate supervisor on her last day. Her own rendition of take this job and shove it.

No. Returning to her old job was definitely not an option.

She felt hands on her feet. Hot, probing hands. She shot to a sitting position and gaped at Joe, who was crouched beside the bed. "What are you doing?" she whispered. It wasn't supposed to be a whisper. But that's what it ended up being as he took one of her sandals off and ran a fingertip along her overly sensitive arch.

He offered a grin, then dragged his fingers along the length of her size-eight foot. Ripley gasped as a shiver wound up and around her, seeming to touch every one of her nerve endings.

"What's the matter, Ripley? Are you ticklish?"

In all honesty, she couldn't have said. No one had tried to tickle her before. Her parents hadn't been the touchy-feely type. And certainly none of her boyfriends had ever gone near her feet. But given her response to Joe's touch, she'd have to say that she definitely was ticklish, even if laughing was the furthest thing from her mind right then.

She swallowed hard. "Half the grime from Memphis's streets is down there. Doesn't that, um, bother you?"

He slid her other sandal off and worked her foot around and around. "What's a little grime between friends?"

"Friends?"

"Yeah. I'd like to think you're my friend."

Friends.

Ripley sat completely still, staring at him, mesmerized. "Aren't you, um, going to make another crack about what happened back there?" she asked, not liking the thickness of her voice. She sounded too near to tears for her liking. And the last thing she wanted to do was cry. So, all right, she'd mucked up her first case as a private detective. That didn't mean she should throw in the towel, did it?

Or maybe this was one of those signs, like the ones she'd used to change her life around to where it was now. Her meeting Nelson Polk in the park and lapping up his stories about what his life had been like as a P.I. The flyer for a gun range she'd found stuck under her car's windshield wiper. The offering of employee severance packages where she worked. She'd grabbed onto all those signs tightly, telling herself that she was meant to be a private investigator and this was the Fates' way of telling her that.

So what were the Fates trying to tell her now?

"You're wound up tighter than a shoestring," Joe murmured.

"You would be, too, if you just found the person you'd been looking for then lost her again."

She stared into his eyes, finding them bluer than she remembered, darker, somehow, now that they weren't full of irritation or amusement or both. "At least you found her."

She nodded. Yes, she supposed that much was true. She had found Nicole Bennett.

A bit of Nelson Polk wisdom echoed in her mind. "Missing persons cases are the toughest, especially if the missing person doesn't want to be found. Accept that you're lucky to find half of the people you go after. And make sure you get paid up front."

Ripley smiled. If someone as successful as Polk had a fifty percent average, then she supposed she wasn't doing too badly. The smile slowly vanished. Of course, she'd been so excited about landing her first real case that she hadn't followed his second piece of advice. Yes, she'd gotten a two-hundred-dollar retainer, and one fifty toward travel expenses. But the way this case was going, she would be in the hole in no time. And seeing she had no means to contact her client, there was little hope she'd ever see more money. In fact, it was looking like she no longer had a case.

She swallowed hard. "Who am I kidding? I'm not meant for this. I should just pack it all in and go home."

"Home?" Joe asked.

Ripley blinked at him, only then realizing she'd said her thoughts aloud.

"Where's home?"

"St. Louis." She cleared her throat and slid her foot from his grasp, not comfortable with showing him her weak side, even if he did work miracles on her feet. "And you?" she said, trying to steer the conversation away from herself, afraid that if she discussed the possibility of her returning home—giving up before she'd really started—it might become reality.

"Minneapolis," Joe said.

Well, that was a revealing scrap of information, wasn't it? Ripley pulled her bare feet on top of the mattress and wrapped her arms around her knees. Joe sat back against the bed, still on the floor.

"Do you really want to give in?" he asked. "Go home?"

She shrugged, not really sure what she wanted to do just then. And despite her fears, she found she needed to talk about the situation. "It seems the only reasonable, logical thing to do. I mean, the woman who hired me to find a missing person has gone missing herself. Meaning that if I can't find her, too, there's no money...and no client, for that matter." She laid her cheek against her knees, gazing at him. "Then there's the tiny fact that I have no personal interest in finding Nicole Bennett. I mean, even if I had caught her outside the pawnshop, what would I have done with her?"

"Good point."

"Yeah, but not very satisfying." She sighed, then turned her head the other way, away from him, and closed her eyes. "I don't know. Maybe this whole thing, my becoming a P.I., is just pie in the sky. Every day I'm getting closer to the big three-oh. The only thing I know how to do with any amount of success is answer phones and type others' expense reports. My computer science education is probably even obsolete now." She caught her lip between her teeth and bit down hard. "What was I thinking?"

She felt the mattress shift and guessed that Joe had sat on the bed next to her. "Interesting that you should use the word satisfying," he said quietly.

Ripley didn't move, didn't say anything, merely sat there staring at the hotel room wall, trying to ignore that there was a gorgeous, nearly naked man sitting next to her.

"Recently I've been thinking I haven't been getting a lot of satisfaction from my own life."

Fingers slid onto her shoulders. Ripley shivered, realizing he was not beside her, he was behind her. And he was touching her.

"I don't know. I suppose I've been charging full steam ahead for so long that I never stopped to ask myself whether or not I was happy."

She nodded slightly, knowing exactly where he was coming from. That kind of talk was what had gotten her into so much trouble to begin with.

The fingers slid from her shoulders to her back where they kneaded her muscles through her T-shirt. "Mmm, that feels good," she murmured, and closed her eyes.

He didn't respond to her comment, merely continued working his magic with his hands. "I know I've made some cracks here and there about your abilities as a P.I., Ripley," he said quietly, gently moving her hair out of the way and pressing his thumbs to the base of her neck. "But the truth is I admire what you're doing."

She twisted her lips. "Yeah, right. I've done a lot for you to admire. What is it that did it for you? When you caught me hiding under the bed? Or when I practically swallowed a good chunk of pavement when I tripped over my own feet?"

He squeezed her shoulders, and she said, "Ouch."

"Just be quiet and let me finish, will you?" he murmured, his mouth close to her ear.

Air was suddenly at a premium. "Okay."

He continued working the kinks from her muscles. But while the tension eased from certain areas, a different kind of tension began to wind low in her belly.

"Think about it, Ripley. You've done something that a lot of people would never have the guts to do. You took a look at your life midstream, found it lacking, then completely shifted tracks. You quit your old job—"

She made a sound. "I was offered a severance package."

He squeezed a little too hard again, earning a yelp. "I'm talking here, remember?"

She nodded and bit her tongue to keep herself from offering further comment.

"You quit your job—" he paused, waiting to see if she was going to say anything "—and followed your heart."

Yes, she supposed that she had.

"You did something I would never have had the balls to do."

Ripley's heart tripped into a higher gear. She turned her head so she could watch him from the corner of her eye. His expression was thoughtful, intense as he continued his massage. She squinted at him. "But you're successful in what you do—very, if I'm not mistaken."

He grimaced. "Successful doesn't equal happy."

She let go of her legs and sat up. "Do you mind if I take off my T-shirt?" she asked, then went ahead and did it before he could respond.

She was very aware that she wasn't wearing a bra

underneath. She wore the torturous contraptions as seldom as she dared. Of course she'd had no way of knowing that while she was reviewing her case in her old hotel room she would be taking a dip in the pool soon. She drew her knees up and waited. After a moment, she felt Joe's fingertips on her exposed flesh. She shivered at the heat of his touch.

"So, tell me, Joe Pruitt," she said, her voice soft, "what would be the one thing you would do if you could choose anything in the world?"

No immediate response except for the hesitation in his hands. "Is that the question you asked yourself?"

"Uh-huh."

"Dangerous question."

She smiled. "Yeah. I'm proof positive of that."

He didn't respond with words, but his hands seemed somehow hotter, more probing, rubbing her muscles with the skill of a pro, working away the last of her tension and making her feel far too relaxed. Far too turned on.

"So?" she murmured.

His fingers grazed her back then slid to tickle the underside of her breasts. Ripley caught her breath, suppressing a whimper of protest when he returned to her back.

"I don't know," he said finally, thoughtfully. "I'm past my prime for sports to be an option. If they were. And they're not. Not with this knee."

"And I'd like to be a model but, gee, I haven't worn a size two since I *was* two."

His chuckle tickled her skin.

She felt something wet and hot against her back and realized he was kissing her there, right in the middle near her spine. He drew back and blew on the area he'd kissed. She shuddered, and her nipples hardened where she had them pressed against her knees.

"I can tell you what I'd like to do now. Right this minute."

Ripley found her voice. "What?" she asked, though she was pretty sure she already knew the answer.

"Order up room service. I didn't get a chance to finish my lunch."

Ripley threw her head back and laughed so hard she nearly fell off the bed. Joe caught her around the middle, turned her and pressed her into the mattress. Ripley instantly stopped laughing. Her heart thudded unevenly in her chest. The tension in her belly had moved lower, making her throb with want for this man who made her feel like hitting him one minute and kissing him the next.

"Liar," she said.

He stretched out next to her, propping his head on his hand. "Not a liar. A wiseass. There's a difference."

"Oh?" Her gaze slid to the towel he still wore, then her bare midriff. She thought about covering herself with her arms, then stretched her arms out above her head instead, arching her back. She watched his eyes darken as his gaze slid from her eyes to her neck, then finally rested on her bare breasts.

He reached out with his free hand and caught the very tip of her nipple between his thumb and forefinger. He rolled the sensitive stiff flesh then gave a gentle tug. Ripley's back came off the mattress as a rush of heat flooded her inner thighs. He moved his hand to her other breast, using the same massaging technique he'd used on her muscles to bring her nipple even more erect. Then he caught the tip of the breast closest to him in his mouth, and Ripley was sure she had died and gone to heaven.

Suddenly it wasn't enough to be receiving. She wanted to take. Hectic energy filled her to overflowing as she caught his shoulders and pinned him to the bed, straddling his hips. She kissed him restlessly, her hands fumbling for the towel that covered the area she was most interested in.

Joe chuckled softly. "This would work a lot better without the shorts."

Ripley rolled off him, stripped off the shorts in question and followed with the borrowed briefs while he did a search for something on the nightstand table. His wallet for a condom, she realized, her heartbeat kicking up.

This was really going to happen. Here. Now. She was going to have sex with Joe Pruitt. The mere idea was enough to send her lunging for him again.

Since the first moment they met, skin against skin in his hotel bed, she'd felt an electrical shock of attraction. The kind of pull that drew people to rubberneck at car accidents or stare at dead bodies. A dangerous appeal that made you stick around just to see what happened next. Usually nothing did. But Ripley got the distinct impression that something very definitely was going to happen here. And it was going to be damn good.

"Dear Lord," Joe murmured, dragging his mouth from hers and gulping deeply. Ripley felt a thrill that his reaction was due completely, totally, one hundred percent to her.

She smiled at him. "Do what you gotta do, because I'm not waiting anymore."

He squinted at her, the action making his eyes even darker, then scrambled to put on the condom. But when Ripley would have slid down over him, he rolled her over instead so that her back pressed into the soft mattress and his erection pulsed against her slick, swollen flesh.

Oh, boy. Ripley wasn't quite ready for the gaping need that opened in her lower abdomen. A burning ache that begged, yearned to be filled, that she feared might never go away. She wriggled against him restlessly. He smiled at her, spreading her thighs with his knees, then finding the source of her agitation with his fingers. Ripley instantly stopped moving, the breath rushing from her body with that one simple, beautiful move.

"God, are you hot," Joe murmured, running his open mouth down her neck and to her shoulder.

He flicked the hooded bit of flesh at the apex of her thighs with his thumb, and Ripley gasped, automatically thrusting her hips up, seeking a firmer, more satisfying touch.

"Lie still."

That was like waving a tenderloin in front of a hungry lion and telling him to sit. Ripley reached for his hips, wanting to have him inside her...*now*. Needing him to satisfy the ache growing with every leap of her pulse.

"Stop it," he murmured, nipping her ear.

She shuddered and tried to turn her head into his kiss. He grinned and pulled back to gaze into her face.

"You're cruel," she whispered.

"You're hot."

She slid her hand between them and grasped his erection, marveling at the length and width of it. "You're...big."

She'd meant to say that he was hot, too, but the other

word slipped out. He kissed her then, deeply, hungrily. "You're good for the ego, you know?"

"Shut up and let's have sex."

He chuckled, and Ripley laughed, then gasped as he slid two fingers deep inside her. He kissed her open mouth, dipping his tongue inside. "Wow. You're so...warm. So tight."

Ripley caught her bottom lip between her teeth and bit hard, trying to keep herself from flying apart right then. "Joe, if you don't—"

Then he was inside her. All of him. Filling every last inch of the emptiness she'd felt a moment before. "Oh," she murmured, although the word came out as a long moan.

Then he moved. Slowly. Deliciously. As if afraid he might lose the control she was even now frantically holding onto with her fingernails. The friction of his flesh inside hers made her tremble all over, made her thrust her hips up to meet his rather than allow him escape. He groaned and sank deep into her again, robbing her of breath, of movement, rendering her incapable of anything but feeling the sheer ecstasy pounding through her veins, skittering over her skin, hardening her nipples. She curved her legs around his hips and squeezed, holding him tight against her, not caring about the world beyond the bed or the really crappy state of her life right now, only wanting the feelings raging inside her to stay there forever.

Then he withdrew nearly all the way and rocked against her again and the emotions expanded to the tenth power. The next time he withdrew, she let him go without resistance, deciding that, boy, did he know what he was doing. He rolled into her again...and again...and Ripley found his rhythm, clenching her leg muscles then unclenching them, her fingers digging into the taut muscles of his shoulders, her mouth mindlessly seeking and finding his as his arousal reached pleasure spots she didn't know were there.

"So...good," she whispered against his mouth, the tips of her nipples brushing his chest.

Then he murmured something, curses, she thought, and he increased the speed of his thrusts. Ripley gasped and grabbed the blanket on either side of her with both hands, seeking a levity she was quickly losing, trying to stop the world from spinning.

Too late. The explosion in her belly was so overwhelming, so beautiful, her back came up off the mattress, meeting Joe's suddenly still form, straining against him.

Minutes later, Ripley's heart still felt as if it might beat straight out of her chest. She tested her legs by tightening them around Joe's waist, gasping as another spasm ripped through her. He lifted his head where it was buried in the pillow beside her. His grin was all too enticing.

She cleared her throat. "Had I known that was what I was missing, I would have let you have your way the first time I crawled into your bed."

He kissed her. "No, you wouldn't have."

"You're right. I wouldn't." She ran her fingers lazily up and down his back. "But it's nice to think about, isn't it?"

She felt his erection twitch inside her, and his grin told her it wasn't involuntary. "Oh, I think actually doing it blows that one right out of the water."

Ripley threaded her fingers through the damp hair on his head and ground her hips against him. His eyes darkened, all laughter gone. She smiled. "I think you're right."

He tilted his head and kissed one side of her mouth, then the other. "I knew you'd come around to my way of thinking sooner or later." He began to withdraw, and she thrust upward again. "Am I ever glad it was sooner...."

# 7

JOE LAY BACK, caught in that state between sleep and wakefulness, taking more comfort than he probably should in the warm, female body curving against his. Early evening sunlight filtered through the white sheers at the window. No balcony this time. He'd made doubly sure of that when he'd called Gloria to reserve a room. If she'd been puzzled by his request, she didn't indicate. Her hands-off approach was exactly the reason he'd hired her. His mother's wanting to run his personal life was enough to handle. He enjoyed that Gloria stuck to strictly professional, although she wasn't above shocking him with an occasional off-color joke.

Ripley shifted beside him. Joe lazily turned his head, watching her through half-lidded eyes as she carefully, very slowly slid away from him and off the bed. In one sweep, her T-shirt covered her delectable back. But her round bottom was all his to covet as she gathered her shorts and her duffel and made her way toward the bathroom.

"Going somewhere?"

Ripley nearly hit the ceiling, she jumped so high. She turned to face him. "Must you do that?"

"Do what?" he asked, quirking a brow.

"Scare the daylights out of me every chance you get?"

His grin widened. "Every chance I get."

She murmured something under her breath then closed the bathroom door after herself. Joe lay there listening to her taking a shower and tried like hell not to let the afternoon's events completely occupy his thoughts. But it was impossible. Not when he was even now contemplating crawling into the shower with her. If he were convinced she hadn't locked the bathroom door, he'd have made the effort. But though he'd coaxed a sexual openness from her, he was beginning to suspect that a more emotional connection with Ripley would take a little time and a great deal more effort. Call him dumb, but when she'd turned her back and gone silent on him moments after their third mind-blowing bout of sex, he'd considered that an emotional wall.

He pulled the pillow she'd used across his face and breathed in her scent. He detected a bit of chlorine from their dip in the pool earlier, but beneath that lay the peachy scent he was coming to associate solely with her.

He told himself he was a sorry bastard and forced himself to put the pillow on the other side of the bed, just in time to find her staring at him from the bathroom door.

"What are you doing?" she asked, the brush she was using on her wet hair hovering above her head.

"Trying to smother myself. Why? You have a problem with that?"

A quirk of her lips indicated she was about to smile. Good. That was good. At least he hadn't totally spooked her.

He ran his hand over his face. "What is it about

women that they always go into this silent, contemplative mode after sex?"

Ripley gaped at him, the brush again in her hair, where it stayed as she apparently tried to find a response to fit the emotions drifting across her pretty face. "What is it about men that they have to lump every woman they've ever slept with together after sex?" She walked into the bathroom, and a moment later he heard a hair dryer switch on.

"Shit," Joe murmured, throwing the sheet off. He supposed he deserved that. Had she compared him to anyone else, especially after they'd just had sex, he'd have been injured, too.

He pulled on a pair of jeans he always kept stashed in the trunk of his car to change into when he found himself going straight from work to a more casual event. Then he stepped, barefoot, to the door of the bathroom. He leaned against the jamb and watched her declare war on all that glorious auburn hair.

"Sorry," he said.

She notched up the speed of the dryer. "Huh?" She shook her head. "I can't hear you."

He pulled the hand holding the dryer away from her ear and yelled, "I said I'm sorry."

She made a face at him. "You can say that again."

He grimaced and crossed his arms, watching her until she nearly fried her hair to a crisp. Finally, she had to shut the damn thing off. Not that she acknowledged him as she slipped the pistol into the holder. Instead she turned and went to battle with the unruly curls surrounding her face.

"Do you plan on talking to me ever again?"

She shrugged almost petulantly, and he felt his grin beg for a return. "I haven't decided yet."

Joe swiped the brush from her hand. He moved to stand next to her and began brushing his hair.

She snatched the brush back, but even the irritated reaction was better than none at all. "You've probably got dandruff or something."

"Considering that all my stuff is at the other hotel, I figure you getting my dandruff is the least you can do for me."

"No, thanks."

She tried to pass him, but he blocked the door. She rolled her eyes then stared at him. He realized she'd exchanged her T-shirt and shorts for a clingy red dress that hugged her in all the right places and made him wonder what she did or didn't have on underneath the short skirt.

"Where are you going?" he asked, twirling an errant curl around his index finger.

She avidly watched the movement, then licked her lips. "Out."

He chuckled. "I guessed that. Where?"

She ducked under his arm and away from him. He turned and followed her into the room. She sat on the bed and rifled through her duffel bag, pulling out first one strappy sandal, then a second. Another pair of shoes that would torture her feet.

"I thought I'd go back to the pawnshop. I never did get to see what Nicole was doing in there earlier."

"They're closed."

She glanced at him. "They're open till eight." She smiled. "Nice try, though."

He shrugged, did up his jeans, then reached for the polo shirt he always kept with the jeans. Her movements as she laced up the sandals slowed, and he knew she watched him as he pulled the cotton over his head, then tucked it into the waist of his jeans. It was comforting that she felt the same way about him as he did about her. Basically he wanted to jump back into that bed and continue where they'd left off.

"I'll come with you."

She pushed from the bed, tested the sandals, then grabbed her purse. He grimaced as she worked to fit her 9mm into the small clutch purse that obviously carried very little, the gun a huge, obvious bulge inside the black leather. "Is that such a good idea? Um, you wouldn't want that thing to accidentally go off or anything."

She smiled at him and breezed on by. "Don't worry. If it goes off, and you get hit, it'll be completely on purpose." She opened the door and leaned against it. "So are you coming, or what?"

RIPLEY STOOD at the dusty counter of the pawnshop, her gaze flicking every now and again to the grimy window and the empty street beyond. Dusk had fallen, painting the shabbier part of town with edge-smoothing hazy purples and yellows, covering the smaller scars and lending a mystical, almost sentimental quality to some of the larger ones.

She glanced at Joe, who was gawking at men's watches at a counter behind her. "It's a Rolex," she heard him a mutter. "A real one."

"That it is, my man. You want a closer look?" a voice from the back said.

Ripley shifted restlessly from foot to foot as the owner she'd met on her previous visit came out and made his way toward Joe instead of her. She drummed her fingertips on the scratched glass countertop and waited. It took far longer than it should have, considering they'd come here for information, not to shop for high-end timepieces. She sighed and tucked her hair behind her ear, about to say something, when Joe turned, something other than a watch in his hand.

She crossed to stand in front of him, staring at the ornately decorated box he held. Measuring about nine by four by four, the exterior was covered in plush red velvet, semiprecious jewels secured like upholstery pins in a pretty pattern along the sides and top. He popped open the lid.

"Is this it?" Ripley asked, looking at what lay inside. "Is this what Nicole sold?"

The guy behind the counter crossed his arms. "Along with the other two-bit pieces of silverware you saw yesterday. Nobody wants silverware with someone else's initials on it. I haven't had time to inventory and appraise this stuff yet, so what you see is exactly the way she left it."

Ripley fingered a necklace that looked suspiciously like large diamonds mounted in gold, then pulled it out. She wasn't a pro at this, not yet, but she found it odd that Nicole had chosen the pawnshop for loot of this sort. Wouldn't a jeweler be more appropriate?

"Oh they're real, all right," the owner pointed out. "One hundred percent, top of the line zirc."

Cubic zirconia.

Ripley's cheeks went hot. "Oh."

Joe handed her the box and turned toward the owner to barter the price of the lot. Ripley absently stepped to where she'd been standing before, glancing through the box's contents. There were several pieces nestled inside the red velvet, each piece prettier than the one before it. She hadn't been aware they made such quality knockoffs. She glanced through the window, realizing that she and Joe were clearly outlined in the bright interior light. A cab pulled to a stop at the opposite curb, and the back door opened. Ripley stepped nearer the window as a woman's leg appeared, then the rest of her.

Her heart skipped a beat. Nicole's sister.

Gripping the box, she started for the door, then stopped, her gaze colliding with Clarise Bennett's. Thank God she was here. Now that Ripley had recovered the goods Nicole had filched and could report on having seen Nicole in the flesh, maybe she'd get paid.

But rather than head toward her, as was expected, seeing as she'd hired her to do a job a couple days ago, Clarise scrambled into the cab, and the car screeched away from the curb.

"Oh, boy."

Ripley rushed outside, saw the cab turn the first corner, then hurried inside to find Joe still haggling with the pawnshop owner over the price of the box. "Come on!"

She grabbed his arm and tried to tow him toward the door. "Hurry!"

"Hey. You're not going anywhere until you cough up the box or the money," the owner said.

Joe took a handful of bills out of his back pocket and slapped them on the counter, nearly missing it as Ripley dragged him toward the door, then through it. "Keep pulling on me like that, and you'll turn around to find yourself holding an arm with nothing attached."

Ripley glanced at him. "At least it would be moving faster than you are. Come on, Pruitt, get the lead out."

Finally they were in his car and with a jolt and a roll they were taking the same corner as the cab. Joe stared at her. "Do you have any idea how much I had to pay that guy in there?"

"Never mind that," she said. "My client is..." She stared down each of the streets they passed. "There! Back up, back up! Turn there."

"Your client?"

She nodded emphatically, clutching the box in her hands for dear life.

Joe sighed next to her, jammed on the brakes, slammed the car into reverse then made the turn. "Don't tell me. She's running from you, too?"

She spared him an exasperated glance. "Save the gibes for later, will you? We have to catch her."

"And what do we do when we do?"

She blinked at him, her plans not having gone that far. "Why, ask her why she's running from me, of course."

"And get the money I just dropped on that worthless piece of crap you're holding."

Ripley glanced at the item in question. She ran her fingers over the top of it, then opened the lid again. Why would Clarise Bennett go through all this trouble to find a boxful of costume jewelry? And what did the FBI—allowing that they were, indeed, FBI—want with it?

"I don't like this." Joe muttered the words she was thinking. "Something smells very fishy. And it has nothing to do with the Mississippi looming ahead."

Ripley snapped her gaze up to find that they were, indeed, near the Mississippi. The cab made a quick right.

"Hurry! Don't lose her!"

He cursed under his breath, then made the turn. Ripley blinked and stared at the giant glass pyramid they were nearing, the sun's last rays reflecting off the structure like it was some sort of mystical aberration nestled between the banks of the Mississippi and the city's modern skyline. "God, she's going to the Pyramid."

"A little late to take in the Egyptian exhibit, don't you think?" Joe asked quietly.

"Public place. Nelson told me they always head for a public place. Much easier to get lost in a sea of other people." She scanned the stairs leading to the front entrance as Joe followed the taxi up the drive. The ground-level exit doors on the side of the Pyramid Arena opened, and people began spilling out.

"Who in the hell is Nelson?" Joe asked.

"Huh?"

"You just said Nelson told you they always head for a public place."

She snapped the box closed and waved her hand. "Nelson Polk. He's, um, he's a friend." Now was not the time or the place to go into detail about who Polk was and why he had given her advice. "The cab's stopped."

But, unfortunately, they weren't anywhere near it. Ripley was on the edge of her seat as Joe maneuvered around a stopped vehicle, then another, trying to catch up to the taxi while Ripley glued her gaze to the woman hurrying from the back. She tucked the curious box under the passenger seat then reached for her door handle. She glanced at what she was wearing. *Figures.* One of the few times she decided to wear heels and a dress, and she had to chase someone. Not that it mattered. She was in shorts and a T-shirt earlier and tripped over her own feet.

She only wished she knew why the woman who had hired her was running from her.

Joe pulled into the spot the taxi just vacated, and Ripley hit the pavement, running after Clarise with all the speed her four-inch heels would allow her. Which, it turned out, wasn't very fast at all. She bumped into one person then another, exiting the building, as she made her way to the door Clarise had disappeared into. Puffing for air, she glanced back to find Joe arguing with a guard. She rushed headlong into someone and nearly knocked the other woman right to the ground.

"Sorry, excuse me," she said, continuing her maze-like route for the entrance that only seemed to get farther away.

She finally reached the door and tried to duck inside. A guard caught her by the arm. "The Pyramid is closing," he said, staring at her.

Ripley caught her balance, staring at him in breathless exasperation. "I left my purse inside," she offered by way of explanation. "Please. It will only take a second. I know right where I left it."

The excuse was working. Well, at least until he caught a glimpse of the bag she was trying to hide behind her back.

He grinned at her. "Nice try, lady. Look, you're just going to have to hold it until you get home. I can't let you in."

Ripley ridiculously felt like stomping her feet and throwing a tantrum. Clarise had gone in there not two minutes ago and didn't appear to have a problem. Why was she being singled out?

"Problem?" Joe appeared at her elbow, eyeing the guard who still held her arm.

The guard released her. "No entrance."

Ripley watched Joe's chest puff out, even though the

guard had at least a hundred pounds on him. She grasped his arm and smiled at the guard. "Oh, well. I guess I'll just have to wait until we get to the restaurant to use the rest room, won't I, pooh bear?"

Joe cocked a brow at her. Pooh bear? Okay, it had been the best she could do at the moment. She tugged on his arm, pulling him to the side before they got trampled by the exiting hordes. Either that or shot by the guard. She looked at Hulk Hogan and wondered if he was carrying. He had stepped into the shadows to allow a larger exit, so she couldn't tell.

"Are you sure you saw her going inside?" Joe asked, his chest still puffed out.

Ripley smiled at him, unable to suppress the urge to smooth her hand down that magnificent chest barreled in prime confrontation mode just for her. "Positive."

He glanced at her fingers, that dark energy she'd seen so much of that afternoon looming large as life in his blue, blue eyes. "So, um, what do we do now?"

She dropped her hand to her purse and straightened it. "I guess we wait for Clarise to either come out or get kicked out."

"Some plan."

"You got a better one?"

He shook his head. "Nope."

She stood back and scanned the morphing crowd. Now she knew why people eluding capture or being tracked targeted such gatherings. There were so many people, colors and sizes seemed to blend together, making it difficult to spot a relative much less a woman she'd seen only once. Well, aside from the glimpse outside the pawnshop. And then she hadn't noticed anything more than that Clarise had been wearing a black dress. She squinted at the horizon where the sun had slipped silently down and twisted her lips. This wasn't looking very good. She glanced in the direction of the access road, and her eyes widened.

"Oh, boy."

"What? What is it?" Joe asked, trying to follow her line of vision. "Did you spot her?"

She swallowed. "That guard you were talking to when you parked—what did he say?"

"That he'd have me towed if I left the car there. Why?"

She pointed at a tow truck pulling away from the curb. "I think he just made good on his threat."

Joe stared, then sprung into action, sprinting after the departing truck with the speed of a man who ran regularly. Not that he could have caught up with the vehicle in any case. The battered truck towing his car had gotten the jump on him.

Ripley slipped a pad and pen from her purse, careful not to disturb the gun, and copied the number on the side of the truck. She used to think towing operators put their contact information there for advertising purposes. Now she suspected it was for moments like these.

She stuffed the pad into her purse and pretended an intense interest in her shoes as Joe dragged himself back to stand next to her.

"They towed my car," he said unnecessarily.

"I got the number. We'll call when we get back to the hotel and see where it is."

Joe paced away from her, then back.

"Don't worry," she said, finally looking at the tense expression on his face. "I'll cover everything."

He stopped pacing. "There's one little problem with that scenario, Ripley."

She straightened.

"If those goons this morning really are the FBI, they'll be all over the car."

"Right," she said absently. Then she was pacing alongside Joe, muttering under her breath the same way he was. Forget that they no longer had wheels. The box Nicole had sold to the pawnshop was in the car. A box that possibly held the key to unlock the mess Ripley was currently smack dab in the middle of. A box that she had hoped to dangle in front of Clarise's eyes to get her to spill what was really going on. A box that was sitting under the seat of the car being towed out of the parking lot.

"Damn, damn, damn," she whispered, missing the turn as she paced with Joe and nearly colliding with him when she finally did pivot.

She blinked into his eyes, her nose filled with the manly scent of him. Every sexy minute of the past few hours rushed back to her. She licked her lips, and he followed the movement, making her mouth dryer still.

"Pardon me," she murmured.

"Sorry," he said at the same time.

Ripley watched as he rounded her and continued pacing. She gave up and leaned against the building, crossing her arms over her stomach.

Could anything else possibly go wrong during the course of this case? She'd nearly been snowed under with the hopelessness of it all earlier. Then she'd found her legs again after incredible sex with Joe, and now here she stood, right back at square one.

Twenty minutes later, darkness completely cloaked the area in which they stood, and the ceaseless column of people...well, ceased. Ripley stared, unsurprised, when the large door was closed with a dull clang and a key was turned in the lock. Joe had stopped pacing and was standing next to her, his arms crossed over his chest in the same way hers were. A few cars remained in the gargantuan, well-lit parking lot, probably belonging to the maintenance and security crew. Otherwise the place was completely deserted.

Ripley tucked her hair behind her ear. "She must have gotten past us."

"Yeah," Joe muttered. He glanced at her, clearly irritated. "So now what do you suggest?"

She dropped her gaze. "I don't know."

He sighed, then ran his hand over his face. He looked at her. "Don't even think about busting into that place and checking the rest rooms."

She smiled. "The thought hadn't even crossed my mind."

"Good."

"Fine."

"Perfect."

"Wonderful."

His grimace turned into a half smile. "Do you always have to get in the last word?"

"Always."

His gaze flicked over her face, lingering on her mouth.

Ripley ignored the instant fire that ignited in her belly and rolled her eyes. "I'm not even going to ask what your suggestion is."

"What? That we go back to the hotel room, forget about your missing person and missing client and become reacquainted with the bed?"

She pointed a finger at him and pushed from the wall. "Why did I know you'd say that?"

"Because you're thinking the same thing?"

Maybe. But she wasn't going to tell him that. She liked his handsome head the size it was. She turned toward the hulking pyramid and started walking on the off chance that Clarise was even now slinking from one of the other exits. She turned the corner and stopped dead in her tracks.

"Why are you following me?" a female voice asked, two hands holding a gun pointed directly at Ripley's stomach.

# 8

NICOLE BENNETT.

Ripley stared directly into face of the very woman she'd been sent to find but who instead had found her, trying to ignore the size and nearness of the gun Nicole held tightly in both hands.

Yet another first in what was adding up to a whole series of them.

"I'll repeat, just in case you didn't hear me. Why are you following me?" Nicole took a step back when Joe rounded the corner at full throttle.

Ripley put her arm out to stop him, and he held up his hands and said, "Whoa."

Ripley wondered how long it would take to get her gun out of her bag. Judging that it had taken her five minutes to get the sucker in there, it would probably take at least that long to get it out. And somehow she didn't think pointing her black leather bag at Nicole and yelling, "Freeze," was going to work, either.

"We're not following you," Ripley said. She shifted, agitated. "I mean, I am...was looking for you, but I'm not now."

Nicole Bennett was prettier than the grainy picture Clarise had given her. With long dark, almost black hair, and wide gray eyes, she was strikingly beautiful and very dangerous. The fact that she had a gun pointed at Ripley could very well have a lot to do with the latter description.

"Say that again?" Nicole asked.

Ripley tucked her hair behind her ear. "Look, I'm a P.I. from St. Louis. I was hired to find you by someone concerned for your welfare."

Nicole's expression was clearly skeptical, but she nodded. "Go on. I'm listening."

Ripley nodded. "Your sister. She wanted me to find you, and the things you, um, borrowed from her."

Nicole narrowed her eyes, but the gun never budged. "Interesting. My sister is in a sanitarium."

Ripley blinked at her. "Well, then, she was released. Because I met her. She gave me a picture of you, told me you have a habit of lifting things from her house, but that she never pressed charges, and asked me to find you." She frowned. "Your name is Nicole Bennett, isn't it? And your sister is Clarise Bennett."

The other woman was not looking very sociable. "Describe the woman who hired you to find me."

Joe leaned closer to Ripley. "Remember that fishy feeling I had earlier?"

Ripley elbowed him in the ribs. "She, um, has blond hair. About your height. No, a little taller. Slender. Kind of a Grace Kelly look-alike with an edge."

The gun dropped to the woman's side, and she shocked the hell out of Ripley by smiling. "That's what I thought," she said. She opened her black trench coat and slid the revolver into the waist of an equally dark pair of slacks, then covered the gun with the hem of her black mock turtleneck. "Did you find the stuff?"

"By stuff, I'm assuming you mean the box you sold to the pawnshop?"

"That's it."

"Yes, I retrieved it." Ripley stared at Joe, warning him not to say the same box was on its way to a holding lot even as they spoke.

"Good." She glanced one way, then other. "Give it to...my sister."

Ripley grimaced at her. "Well, that's the problem. It seems your sister is now also running from me. In fact, we followed her here."

"Here?" Nicole looked suddenly antsy and mumbled something under her breath.

"Yes. That's what I meant when I said we weren't following you. We were following her. Here."

Nicole began backing away, her expression wary as she scanned the area surrounding them. "Just make sure she gets that box."

She turned and began hurrying away.

Ripley grabbed her purse, reaching for the gun in it, and started after her. "Hey, wait a minute!" she called. She supposed she should be glad she hadn't yelled, "freeze," although in her book, "Wait a minute" ranked right up there alongside it.

Joe grasped her wrist. "What are you doing?"

"Going to get some answers, of course."

Joe shook his head. "I don't think that's a very good idea."

"That's funny, did you hear anyone asking for your opinion? I didn't." Ripley had just had a gun held on her by a woman she had been searching for but who had found her instead, and Joe wanted her to pass up the opportunity to get answers to the questions mounting in her brain?

He released her.

She turned. Only to find that Nicole Bennett had disappeared into thin air.

THE FOLLOWING MORNING Ripley pored over the contents of the too-thin case folder strewn across the bed in front of her, staring at the photo of Nicole Bennett, checking out the information Clarise Bennett had given her and trying to piece it together with what had gone down so far. She sighed and collapsed against the pillows, suddenly all too aware that the king-size hotel bed seemed big and awfully empty without Joe in it.

She poked a sheet of paper aside with her toe and reprimanded herself. She and Joe were not a couple. She didn't even want a relationship right now, much less one with an uptight and overbearing albeit super sexy shoe salesman who had sex on the brain.

She turned her head to stare at his pillow. They'd had more of that great sex last night after getting back from the Pyramid. Well, not directly afterward. There had been the hour-long period where she tried to fit the puzzle pieces together and he questioned her sanity, but the instant she'd climbed into bed and turned her back, he was right in there alongside her. And the more she told herself she was not going to have sex with him again, the more her body rebelled, responding to the feel of his hot body pressing against her. She'd eventually given in and arched into him, and that had clinched it. They'd had sweaty, hot, wild monkey sex all night long.

Ripley rubbed her fingertips against her forehead and stared at the door he'd disappeared through. He had said he was going to scare up some doughnuts. She didn't need four days of detective experience to figure out it didn't take nearly an hour and half to get them.

She supposed that when all was said and done, Joe was being a pretty good sport about all of this. After all, it wasn't every day that you woke up to find a strange naked woman in your bed, got chased from your second-story hotel room and dropped into a pool, had your car towed, then, as if all that wasn't enough, had a gun pulled on you by the very woman you had been looking for, but hadn't been looking for that minute.

Then again, she supposed it could be the sex.

But a guy like Joe...well, he could pretty much have any woman he wanted. He had it going on and then some in the looks department. And his sense of humor had her smiling even if she did want to sock him one when that acerbic wit was turned on her.

And what about her? Why was she hanging around with Joe when she should be concentrating on her new career and figuring out what had gone wrong with her first case?

She smiled. "Very definitely the sex."

She sat up and hung her legs over the side of the bed. She'd always thought the intimate act highly overrated. She'd dated and had sex with three men before Joe. First had been Jack Basset in the back seat of his father's Chevy after the senior prom, when she'd been left deflated and unfulfilled while he got out, his skyblue suit pants hanging open as he cheered from the hood of his car. Number two had been Terry Sheen in college. He hadn't owned a Chevy, but he had been a quick finisher. So fast, in fact, she wondered if what they'd had was really sex or more like a series of hit-and-run episodes, with more running involved than hitting.

Then, of course, there was the guy behind door number three. She should have had Monty Hall close the door on him and opted for the lifetime supply of laundry detergent instead. Whoever said size didn't matter? Well, they'd never slept with Tiny Tim Bensen. And here she had thought they jokingly called him Tiny because he was six foot four, two hundred pounds. Little did she know.

Ripley laughed, unable to believe she was thinking of her sex life in such a lighthearted manner. It wasn't so long ago—two days, in fact—that she had questioned her own sexuality as a result of those same three men, thinking it was her fault she had never achieved orgasm during sex. She'd never even imagined that the problem had been the guys, that they hadn't been able to keep up with her.

Then came Joe.

She got hot just thinking about him. Was it ever nice to know that sex's reputation was well deserved. While she suspected even former jock Joe might have the urge to climb onto the rooftop with his jeans open and shout the news of their great sex to the entire population of Memphis, he stuck around to make sure she was having at least as much fun as he was. And oh, boy, was she ever. Places were sore that she hadn't even known could get sore. And every time she took a step, she was prompted to wonder if there might be such a thing as too much great sex.

Naw...

She gathered her papers, straightened them, then put them into the plain manila folder. Well, that was productive, wasn't it? She'd sat down to figure out the case and instead ended up thinking about Joe. She'd suspected there had to be some drawbacks to what was happening between her and Joe. But for some reason she hadn't equated a very good sex life with a sucky professional one.

Of course, she couldn't help but realize that both Joe and the case had a time clock ticking on them. There was only so long she could continue to pursue a case that she was now officially paying out of pocket to solve instead of the other way around. And Joe...well, as soon as she went home to St. Louis, he was—

The lock on the door clicked. Ripley stared at it. She started when someone tried to open it, stopped by the security latch.

"Ripley, it's me," Joe said, knocking.

She let out the nervous breath she was holding and padded to the door. A moment later he stood inside, the latch firmly in place, grinning at her like he'd been gone days instead of ninety minutes...and like he was very happy to see her.

He held up a bag, and Ripley snatched it from him, opening it before she even returned to the bed.

"A thank-you would be nice."

She fished out a whipped-cream-filled éclair and wrapped her mouth around it, humming with approval. "Thank you," she said with her mouth full.

Joe shook his head and put another bag on the table. "Just save me one, will you?"

Ripley looked in the bag. Five éclairs left. She didn't know if she'd have the strength to leave him any.

"Better yet, give me one now." He stood next to the bed and held his hand out. She put the bag in it, then changed her mind, took it back and handed him one éclair instead. She smiled at him, dipping her tongue out to lap cream from her bottom lip.

Joe very obviously had a difficult time swallowing. "Maybe this wasn't such a good idea."

"It was a great idea." She moved the file then patted the bed beside her. "So tell me."

"Tell you what?" He did a move that left him bouncing on the mattress, legs crossed. Ripley saved the file from falling to the floor.

She swallowed and reached for the coffee he was handing her from the night table. "I know it doesn't take that long to get a couple of doughnuts, Joe."

He grinned at her. "Did you miss me?"

*More than you'll know.* "Nope."

He leaned over and pressed a kiss to her bare knee. "Liar."

She laughed and wriggled away from him, heat blazing up the inside of her thigh straight to the area that would like to be kissed. "Never come between a woman and her doughnuts. You're risking serious injury." She took another bite. "So give."

He ate his doughnut first. Very slowly. Ripley fidgeted as she dug into her second éclair. Okay, so the guy had been raised with manners. But she didn't think talking with his mouth full was what he was worried about right now.

"I went to the tow yard."

She raised her brows.

"Yeah. The car's stored behind eight-foot fences with two very hungry-looking dogs running around loose inside." He frowned and took a slug of coffee from her cup, then handed it back to her. "And another familiar car full of stooges sitting outside."

Ripley had trouble swallowing. "They were there?"

"Yep. All three of them."

"Great." She collapsed against the pillows and sank down, not really thinking about the fact that she wore nothing but a T-shirt and panties. At least until Joe's gaze caught on the patch of cotton between her legs.

"Hmm. Yeah...great."

Ripley tugged on the hem of her T-shirt and covered the area in question. She didn't want to be distracted by sex right now, no matter how much her body responded to his simple suggestive words. "Did anyone ever tell you that you have a one-track mind?"

He grinned at her. "Yeah. You."

"Besides me."

He thought for a minute, then crossed his fingers over his flat, cotton-covered stomach. "Nope. You're the first."

Ripley's stomach tingled. "You're lying."

"And you're beautiful." He reached over her for the bag of doughnuts. She moved it out of the way and smiled at him around another mouthful.

"You're not really thinking about eating all those?"

She swallowed. "Why not?"

"Because you'll get fat."

She whacked him in the arm then tossed him the bag. "One more. That's it."

He grinned and took out another one. "Okay, have it your way. But I think we're going to have to come up with some inventive ways to burn off those calories."

Ripley licked her fingers then wiped her hands on the napkin he supplied. "I think we already did."

"Doesn't count. You have to exercise after the, um, calories." His gaze had drifted suggestively to the hem of her shirt again. She smiled and pushed from the bed.

"Nice try."

She picked up the file from the bed and went to the table, away from temptation in the shape of Joe Pruitt. She opened the folder and fanned the documents.

He sighed in exaggerated exasperation. "Well, since sex is not in my immediate future, you mind tossing me that bag next to you?"

She absently grabbed the bag he'd left on the table when he came in and threw it to the bed, then sat down to concentrate on the case. She ignored the rustle of plastic coming from the bed and her curiosity about what else Joe had bought and stared at the closed file. There had to be something she was missing. What was it?

First off, she was reasonably convinced that there was no blood connection between Nicole and Clarise. She questioned if Bennett was their real name. When she'd arrived in Memphis, the first hotel attendant she'd dropped a twenty on had told her Nicole had checked in under the name Kidman. *Har, har,* she remembered thinking at the time. But if she was going around using false names, then it was possible that Bennett wasn't her real name, either.

She picked up the phone and put a call through to her cousin three times removed on her father's side who worked at the phone company in St. Louis. Janet was two years younger than she was and wasn't the brightest, but they'd always gotten along. After the normal amount of chitchat, she asked Janet to check and see if there was a listing for a Clarise Bennett in the St. Louis or surrounding area. Shocker of shockers, there wasn't. Then she asked her cousin whose name was connected to the number Clarise had given her that was now out of service. Janet seemed a little put off by that one.

"Geez, Ripley, you know I can't do that. That's illegal."

Ripley bit her tongue, stopping herself from saying that's exactly the reason she had called her instead of Information. Ripley rested her chin in her palm, trying to think up an inventive story that would get her what she was looking for. She found one. She told Janet she was going out with this guy, and that was the number he had given her, but he suddenly up and disappeared. The kicker was, she was afraid he was married.

Boy, was she ever going to hear it from her mother once that news made it back to her.

"The name on that account is Christine Bowman," Janet said a moment later. "Only after the initial installation two months ago, she never paid her bill, and the company cut off service a couple of days ago." She made a low sound, then read off the address. Ripley wrote it down. "Swanky. Funny how she could afford a place like that but couldn't make the phone payment." Her voice lowered. "You think that's the wife?"

"Wife?"

Oh, yeah. She'd forgotten her story. "Just as I expected. The no-good, low-down rodent."

She thanked her cousin, then hung up. Was Clarise Bennett really Christine Bowman? She'd bet she was. But why go through all the trouble of giving a false name?

She thought about the story she'd just fed to her cousin. She realized Clarise, aka Christine, had probably fed the sister story to her in order to find Nicole Bennett. But why?

She picked up the photo of Nicole and squinted at it. She wondered at the odd angle again, and the grainy quality. While she'd questioned why it looked like it had been taken from a security camera before, now, armed with the suspicion that Nicole and Christine, aka Clarise, weren't related at all, she was convinced it *had* been taken from a security camera. She leaned closer, examining the surroundings. The shot had been taken on the front steps of a house with white columns flanking the steps and a brick sidewalk snaking beyond them. Nicole wore a simple light-colored dress—it was difficult to tell what color because the shot was in black and white—that looked more like a uniform than your run-of-the-mill dress.

Ripley sat back, thinking.

Okay, so Nicole wasn't Clarise's sister. And Nicole hadn't been at Clarise's house for a regular family visit, either. Ripley suspected Nicole had been working at the house, and not for very long, at that, if Clarise had just moved in a couple months before. Then Nicole had stolen the box....

She crossed her legs. But why then wouldn't Clarise have called the police and reported the items stolen? Why, instead, did she hire Ripley to find Nicole and recover what appeared to be nothing but a boxful of worthless costume jewelry?

She took a deep breath then let it out, the answers she found only sprouting more questions.

"I need that box," she said aloud.

She looked at Joe who lay across the bed, reading a book he had open on his washboard stomach. She ignored the little skip her heart gave then crossed to sit on the bed next to him. "What are the chances of our getting into the car without anyone noticing us?"

He laid the book, cover down, on his stomach and glanced at her. "Oh, about zero to none."

"Not the answer I was looking for."

"Unfortunately it's the only one I've got for you."

She snuggled a little more comfortably against the pillows and fingered the pages of the book. "What are you reading?"

She found it hard to believe he would be reading a novel in the midst of all this. But the truth was she didn't know Joe very well. Maybe he read when he was nervous or in trouble. Lord knew others did far stranger things to calm their nerves. Her mother scrubbed the walls in the entire house when she was worried about something. Ripley eyed the hotel room walls, thinking she'd prefer to read.

He held the book up so she could see the cover.

*How to Become a P.I. In Ten Quick, Simple Steps.*

She gaped at him. "You're kidding."

He grinned. "Nope."

She snatched the book out of his hands and glanced at the back cover. She was familiar with the book. She'd checked a copy of it out of the St. Louis main library a month ago. But what was he doing with it?

She tossed it back to him and sighed. "What are you doing, Joe?"

He closed the book and put it on the nightstand. "I figured I needed something to do when we weren't having sex."

"And your becoming a P.I. is what you came up with?"

He shook his head, his grin making her thighs quiver. "Nope. You're the P.I. I just thought reading up on the subject would make me more of a help than a hindrance."

She lolled her head on the pillow, not sure if she should be touched or insulted. She opted for touched and tried to ignore the other. "So does this mean I have to read up on shoes now?"

He chuckled. "Not unless you want to."

He leaned closer to her, his index finger finding its way to the hem of her T-shirt. "You know, we could skip all the P.I. and shoes stuff and go straight to the sex part."

A thrill raced up her skin, hardening her breasts and making her blood start to simmer. "Hmm," she said, watching as he lifted the hem of her T-shirt and revealed her plain white panties.

"You ever hear of Victoria's Secret?"

She tried to move his hand away. "You ever hear of tact?"

The finger worked its way under the elastic of her panties and lightly stroked her. Ripley gasped, surprised by the instant awakening of all sorts of hot feelings up and down her body.

He withdrew the finger from the bottom of the panties and moved to the top, tugging the cotton down her hips. "We could always eliminate the topic of underwear altogether."

Ripley swallowed hard. "We could."

Down and off went the panties. But instead of coming right back up, Joe took one of her feet in his hands. He did something to her toes that made her nipples ache. Then his long fingers rubbed her instep, sending shivers up her arms and down her back.

"Do you have a thing for feet?" She'd meant the comment as a mild crack, but her voice sounded raspy even to her, betraying how very much she liked what he was doing.

He grinned and ran a fingertip from heel to toe, eliciting a shallow gasp. "Feet are my business."

She caught her bottom lip between her teeth. "Some men are breast men. Others leg men. Just my luck that I'd pick a guy with a foot fetish."

His chuckle tickled the sensitive skin on her leg, making her realize he'd graduated from her feet and was making his way up her body.

Ripley settled a little more firmly on the mattress,

stretching her neck when his fingers found her magic button and began stroking it.

"God, you're so hot," Joe murmured, the air from the words stirring the hair between her legs.

Ripley cracked open her eyes just as his mouth pressed against her heated core, his thumbs holding her swollen flesh open to his attentions. She gasped, caught between needing to push him away and wanting him to do exactly what he was doing.

Her back arched violently, shamelessly pushing her against him as he laved her with his tongue. She restlessly licked her lips, thinking a girl could definitely get used to this. He sucked her most sensitive piece of flesh, and she shuddered. Oh, yeah...definitely.

Up and up she soared. She was teetering on the precipice...when Joe removed his mouth.

"No!" she cried, trying to force him back down.

He chuckled, and a moment later her protests left her when his mouth was replaced by his arousal, thick and hard and pulsing between her legs. She thrust her hips against his.

"Impatient this morning, aren't we?" he murmured, nipping the flesh at the base of her neck.

"Just shut up and give it to me."

He ran his shaft the length of her flesh then back again. "Give you what, Ripley? I want to hear you say it."

She blinked her eyes open to stare at him, her breath rushing from her lungs at the raw, undiluted need on his face.

She reached down and gripped his length in her fingers, giving a squeeze for good measure, and finding him sheathed in a condom. She fit the knob of his arousal against her opening, then thrust her hips quickly upward. "This...oh, yes, this..."

# 9

THE MORE SEX THEY HAD, the more sex Joe wanted.

Ripley wriggled beneath him, and he rocked into her to the hilt, taking great pleasure in her shudders, the sway of her breasts, the bowing of her lips as she pulled in quick, shallow breaths. He claimed her mouth, running his tongue along the length of her lips, then thrust again.

Who knew it could be this good?

The emotions raging through him were both familiar and foreign. He'd had sex with his share of women, but the burning need that always invaded his groin roared through his entire body when he was getting sweaty with Ripley. He stopped short of thinking they were a perfect fit, but when her slick muscles contracted around him, he felt like the most important man on earth. Like this was the place he was meant to be, and he never wanted to leave it. Before...well, he had been after only one thing—his own gratification. And it wasn't simply that he was concerned with Ripley's pleasure, it was also that he didn't want their physical coming together to end. And pleasuring her helped ensure that it wouldn't.

He ran his fingers over her breasts, then between the two globes of flesh, wondering at the dampness there, then moved his hands beneath her to cup her bottom, fitting her to him even more closely. She protested the lack of freedom, and he kissed her words away, reluctantly sliding his hands from her bottom and down her thighs, curving her legs until they were bent between them. When he thrust this time, she called out his name and shattered beneath him. He watched the myriad expressions cross her face as she climaxed.

He tried to hold back, to enjoy merely watching her. But just seeing her experience so much pleasure, knowing he could take credit for it, made him explode right along with her.

Moments later, his mouth pressed to Ripley's sweat-dampened neck, he felt a moment of what he was pretty sure was fear. Not fear that he hadn't performed well. Or that his weight was too much for her. Fear that what was happening between them wouldn't last.

Ripley gave a low, husky laugh. "You know, at some point we're going to have to get out of this bed."

He pulled back to gaze into her face, taking in the humor in her eyes, the flushed state of her skin. "Why?"

She took his head in her hands and kissed him fully on the mouth. "Because I have a case to solve."

He couldn't help his grimace. And what happened when she did solve that case? Would she go back to St. Louis? Where would that leave things between them?

For the first time in his memory, probably ever, Joe thought he'd gained an insight into what went through the minds of those women who desperately tried to cling to him after sex. And it wasn't a pretty picture.

Ripley pushed at his shoulders, and he reluctantly rolled off her, watching as she headed for the bathroom and the shower.

Joe rubbed both hands against his face, breathing in

the sweet scent of her that lingered there and trying like hell not to feel like an idiot.

He'd spent some time with a woman in Dallas. Once, after they'd had sex and he lay almost indifferent on the other side of the bed, she had told him that one of these days he was going to meet that one person who would make him feel what she was feeling. He'd stopped himself from scoffing at her and listened patiently, but he'd been thinking he was immune to whatever it was that made women turn from perfectly good bed buddies into demanding, commitment-hungry monsters.

He glanced toward the open bathroom door. Unfortunately, he thought he was finding out that not only wasn't he immune, he was feeling whatever that feeling was in spades.

He rolled out of bed, discarded the used condom, then began pacing the length of the room. This wasn't good. This wasn't good at all. This wasn't supposed to happen to *him*.

He caught himself. *Okay, get a grip, guy. So you like having sex with this woman. And you don't want that sex to end just yet.* There was nothing wrong with that. It didn't mean he was falling into the big one. That he'd stuck his foot right in the middle of it.

Love.

No. No. There was a difference between sex and love. He'd learned that in sex ed classes.

And that was exactly the reason he was afraid he was coming to know the other side a little too well.

Ripley came out of the bathroom freshly scrubbed, her auburn curls somewhat tamed. She was dressed in khaki shorts and a white blouse with a white tank top underneath. And she couldn't have looked sexier to him had she been in one of those sheer, body-hugging getups he saw in the Victoria's Secret catalogues that were delivered to his house.

*Holy shit, I am in love with her*, he realized with a breath-robbing gulp.

"Ready?" she asked.

No. Hell, no. He wasn't anywhere near ready. In fact, he'd never be ready. What was he going to do? Where was he going to go? She was watching him. What was he going to say?

"For what?" he forced himself to ask.

"To get the box from the car, of course."

"Of course," he repeated, pacing from one end of the room to the other. He forced himself to stop, to try to gain some perspective, but all he could think of was the terrifying "L" word.

He finally forced himself to put on his clothes, more to distract himself from his thoughts than as a response. Then her words sank in, and he turned to face her even as he tucked his shirt into his jeans. "What did you just say?"

She glanced at him guilelessly from where she was putting her file together. "What? That we're going to get the box from your car?"

"Yes, that's it." He crossed his arms over his chest and tried to ignore how much he wanted to tackle her back to the bed. "Are you insane? There's no way we're getting into that place without those goons seeing us." Or the dogs. He wasn't sure which was worse.

She slung her purse over her shoulder, tucked the file under her arm and headed for the door. "Exactly."

Joe caught the door with his hand, pushing it closed. He eyed the damp tendrils of hair that clung to her finely curved neck. "What do you mean, exactly?"

She shrugged and held the file against her chest. "Nelson told me that there are times when it's wise to make friends out of your enemies."

That Nelson Polk again. Joe sighed.

She smiled. "I think it's time you and I found out who our new friends really are, and what, exactly, they're after."

OKAY, JOE WAS ACTING decidedly weird. Ripley pulled her hair off her neck then fastened it into a loose twist at the top of her head. She'd come out of the shower to find him looking at her in a way she could only describe as shell-shocked. And that seemed to be the general way he'd looked at her since. No wiseass remarks. No trying to get into her underpants. Instead, he appeared ready to bolt in the other direction if she so much as said boo to him.

She smiled, tempted to do just that.

In the back of the taxi she'd called to pick them up, Joe couldn't have sat farther away from her had he tried. And she got the distinct impression he was trying. He all but had the side of his face smashed against the window in his effort to stay away from her.

So she did the natural thing. She reached out and touched him.

He started, and she laughed.

"Am I missing something here?" she asked. She began to remove her hand from his arm, then changed her mind, deciding she liked him being a little ill at ease. At her mercy, so to speak.

She watched him swallow hard then shake his head. "It's just that I don't know if this is such a good idea."

She smoothed her hand up his arm, then over his chest, her fingers seeking and finding the opening of his shirt and slipping inside to tease the fine, crisp hair there. The tension that practically radiated from him was of the anxious variety. She smiled and dipped her fingers down to roll over one of his flat nipples.

He caught her hand. "Would you cut it out? I'm serious here."

That was the thing. He was a little too serious.

Could it be that all this was finally getting to him? That the source of his anxiety stemmed from the three goons they were about to face off with? After all, she could only guess at what had happened when he'd gone head-to-head with them alone.

"There's nothing to worry about, Joe," she said, sitting back on her side of the seat and watching as he collapsed against his side in almost comical relief. "If they are FBI, then we're safe because neither of us has done anything wrong." She hoped. "If they're not...well, it's the middle of the day. What do you think they're going to do? Shoot us?"

"The thought has crossed my mind."

"Well, then, we'll shoot them back." She patted the bag that held her gun for emphasis.

"Gee, that's reassuring." A return of the old Joe, but the words didn't hold half the energy they usually did.

She'd told the driver to let her know when they were getting close. He spoke. She requested he drop them off at the corner opposite the towing yard then gave him a nice tip for his efforts.

She got out of the car and held the door open. "Are you coming?" she asked. Joe didn't seem to be aware the cab had stopped.

He grimaced then climbed out to stand next to her, smoothing his already smooth shirt. The cab drove off, and they both watched it, wrapped up in their own thoughts.

Ripley took his arm and began walking toward the holding lot. There. The sedan holding the three goons sat parked at the curb on the opposite side of the street. Ripley crossed, heading straight for the garage next to the towing lot that probably held the office.

"Where are we going?" Joe asked, blinking at her.

"To get your car back."

"Fine. It's your ass."

He seemed to consider the body part in question as she walked slightly in front of him. She tugged him so he walked even with her. "I don't have a thing to worry about." *I hope.*

With barely a glance at the dark blue sedan, she and Joe entered through the door of the garage, the interior dim and cluttered and looking pretty much like every other garage she'd been in. The only difference was that normally her heart didn't threaten to pound a hole through her chest, and she usually didn't have three goons following her.

Joe stepped up to a caged office where a guy smoking a cigar sat reading the sports section of the newspaper. She supposed he needed protection. Most people didn't take kindly to having their cars towed.

Joe took his license from his wallet, put it in front of the guy and launched into his spiel, while Ripley stood to the side, slipping her hand into her purse. Her fingers met with the cold, unyielding metal of her gun as she watched the door. She quickly snatched her hand out. Who was she kidding? She couldn't shoot a rabid dog if it were charging her. Well, okay, maybe she could. But she wasn't in a hurry to find out. She only hoped these guys weren't foaming at the mouth.

Joe's voice rose, and Ripley blinked to find him arguing with the attendant who stared at him indifferently and shifted the cigar in his mouth with his tongue. She realized the cage was also necessary to enable the occupant to get away with highway robbery.

Joe finally counted out bills one by one and flicked them at the attendant. Ripley calculated the amount, adding it to the running tab she already owed Joe. The sum was starting to eat into a good chunk of her savings, but the guy hadn't breathed one word to her about all he'd given up for her so far. Besides, she owed him more than money.

The door to the outside finally opened, and Ripley wasn't ready for it. She jumped and turned toward it, only to see a woman she didn't recognize step to the cage. Another towing victim? She'd venture a yes. Ripley stepped closer to the door and opened it a crack to peek at the sedan. Still there. Men still inside. She frowned and let the door close again.

"Over there," the smirking attendant said, pointing to another door to the side that probably led to the towing yard. "Just give me a minute to call the dogs in."

Joe said something to him Ripley wasn't sure she wanted to hear, then led the way to the door the attendant had motioned to.

"Hey!" the woman who had come in called after the attendant. "I've got appointments."

"Yeah, well, now you gotta wait," he shouted.

Ripley didn't have to wonder why he'd taken the job. Obviously he enjoyed it.

Joe leaned in closer to her. "Where are our friends?"

"Still outside."

He grimaced.

Her thoughts exactly.

"So what's the plan now?"

She tapped her finger against her lips, considering the situation. She pulled her bag closer to her side, reassured by the weight of it. "Pull the car out on the street and wait for me."

She began to walk away, only to be towed back by the collar of her blouse. "Uh-uh. Not an option."

She wriggled free from his grasp. "That's not for you to say."

"So long as I'm with you, it is."

Ripley scanned Joe's handsome, irritated face, finding the frustration from dealing with the attendant gone and the seriousness back. Then it dawned on her what may be behind the change. "You're worried about me, aren't you?" she asked wonderingly.

She'd never had anyone outside her parents worry about her before. And it felt pretty good. Not that she had given her parents much to worry about. Up until now she'd always done things exactly the way they wanted her to. She figured she must have saved up her bad-girl points and was cashing them all in on this one case.

"No, I'm worried about me," Joe said, though she could see it wasn't true. If he was truly worried about only himself, he would have dumped her a long time ago.

"Uh-huh." She glanced toward where someone rapped on the other side of the door. Joe opened it to stare at the attendant. "In a minute." He closed the door again.

Ripley smiled at him. "You know, he may decide to keep the car if you keep doing things like that."

"Let him." He narrowed his gaze. "What are you going to do?"

She shrugged and glanced at the woman drumming her orange acrylic nails against the counter in front of the cage. "I'm going to walk up to the car and ask them what they want with me."

She thought of Nicole Bennett confronting her and Joe the night before and felt a stab of envy. What she wouldn't give for guts like those. Then again, there was a big difference between a green P.I. with a guy along for the ride and the three goombahs sitting outside.

Joe grasped her hand and tugged her toward the door. "We'll confront them together. Right after I get my car out of this godforsaken lot."

She stumbled through the door after him, a protest on her lips. A protest that died right there when Johnny the attendant pressed a button and the gates opened to reveal the three men in question standing there with their arms crossed over their chests.

RIPLEY SAT in the back seat of the plain blue sedan, one of the goons sitting next to her while another sat in the front seat watching her through the rearview mirror. She bit her tongue to keep from asking them what they ate. Whatever it was, it couldn't be healthy. It wasn't normal for guys to be this big.

She peered out the window to where the third guy was talking to Joe near the front of the car.

She sighed and sat back. "Are you guys really FBI?" she asked, staring at first one then the other.

The one in the front seat reached inside his jacket, then flipped open a wallet over the seat, all without turning. She eyed his identification, wondering if he'd ordered it from the same catalog she'd gotten her P.I. badge from.

He flipped the wallet closed and put it away.

"I've never seen agents that look like you." Of course, she'd never really seen an FBI agent up close and this personal before, period, but they didn't have to know that.

Neither of them said anything.

Ripley sighed again and rolled her eyes. Apparently the only one capable of speech was talking to Joe, leaving her here with Harpo and his clone on steroids. All they needed were handheld horns to blow to indicate yes or no, and they could take their act out on the road.

"You look more like Mob to me," she said, then nearly bit her tongue in two. Neither man moved, but she felt the driver's stare intensify on her via the mirror, something she could only sense because all three of them wore mirrored sunglasses. She crossed her arms over her chest. "Then again, if you were Mob, I don't think you'd be flashing FBI IDs around, would you?" she thought aloud. "You wouldn't have to. The mere suggestion of Mob affiliation would be enough, wouldn't it?"

Someone rapped on her window, and she jumped. She looked up to see goon number three motioning for the door to open. The automatic locks sounded, and he pulled the door open.

"You're free to go, ma'am."

She squinted at him. A Mob guy wouldn't call her ma'am, would he? "Are you sure?"

Did she really just ask that? When someone like him said that you were free to go, you went.

A smile tilted the sides of his mouth then vanished. "Not unless you don't want to."

She couldn't have scrambled from the car faster had she been pushed.

Ripley stood in the middle of the street, gaping as the guy rounded the rear of the car and got into the front seat alongside Tweedledum. Then the sedan drove away from the curb and down the street, turning at the next corner.

Joe came to stand next to her. "Come on, let's go get lunch."

JOE SAT across from Ripley in a rib joint on the edge of Beale Street and grinned at her sudden loss of appetite. He'd had to order for her, because she hadn't said a word since he'd stuffed her stiff body into his car and driven the short way to the infamous street.

They sat in the corner of a bar decorated with old posters of blues legends, donated musical instruments and autographs written directly on the wall. The three-piece band set up near the door played without a singer.

Ripley finally blinked out of her shock-induced coma. "You're telling me he let you go because he's from Minneapolis and remembered you from your college basketball days?"

Joe leaned his forearms on the table. "Yep." Seldom was he reminded of the time he'd spent with the University of Minnesota Golden Gophers. But if he could haven chosen a moment, this would definitely have been one of them.

She rolled her eyes and flopped back in her chair.

"Well, that, and I told him everything I knew about you and the case you're working on." He straightened his napkin.

Her eyes widened.

"And here I thought you'd be happy to find out that you're not in any trouble."

"I already knew that. Sort of. I haven't done anything wrong."

He stared at her. "You wouldn't happen to know a Christine Bowman, would you?"

She blinked at him. "Christine Bowman is Clarise Bennett."

He cocked a brow.

"I found that out this morning when I called to check whose name the contact number Clarise had given me belonged to." She chugged down the water in the glass in front of her, her gaze constantly darting through the window. "So it's Nicole that they want, isn't it?" She looked squarely at him, her chocolate brown eyes wide and wondering. "What did she do?"

"As far as they're concerned, nothing."

"Nothing?"

"It's not her they're after. It's Christine Bowman."

"The woman who hired me?"

He nodded.

"Did they say what they want her for?"

He chuckled and leaned back so the waitress could take his plate. She reached to take Ripley's, as well, but she slapped her hand down on the edge and said she wasn't done, when in truth she had yet to touch it. Joe guessed that her appetite had made a comeback. "It wasn't exactly a give-and-take kind of conversation, Ripley. I did most of the giving, and Agent Miller did most of the taking."

"So they want Christine..." She broke off a rib from the small rack in front of her and rolled an end into a bowl of barbecue sauce. Her gaze suddenly flew to his face. "You didn't tell them about the box, did you?"

He motioned for her to lean forward, and he slowly cleaned a drop of sauce from the side of her mouth with his napkin. He groaned when her tongue dipped out to finish the job.

"No, I didn't tell them about the box," he said, sitting solidly back and out of touching distance.

She seemed to notice his body language, and the tiniest of smiles played around her lush mouth.

He took a business card from his back pocket and held it out to her. "I did, however, promise that we'd contact them if we get any information on either Christine or Nicole."

"Why Nicole?"

"I'm guessing because she might lead them to Christine."

He sat back and watched her dig into her ribs with a vengeance, obviously determined to make up for lost time. He shifted uncomfortably when she made soft, sexy sounds in the back of her throat, the same kind of sounds she made during sex.

"These are the best ribs I've ever had," she murmured before launching another attack on the plate in front of her.

Judging from her slender frame, he'd guess they were some of the few ribs she'd ever had.

"So that's it then?" she asked, finishing in no time flat. Joe glanced around, wondering if they posted a record anywhere. "We don't have to worry about them anymore?"

"We don't need to be jumping from any more balconies, if that's what you mean." He leaned forward and rubbed the back of his neck. "In fact, we can go to the old hotel...you know, if we want."

She stared at him as the waitress removed her plate. "That's good, right? All your stuff's there."

"Yeah," he said. What he didn't say was that returning to the old hotel also meant separate rooms and that there would no longer be a need for them to pretend to be a couple for the purposes of evading the three goons they now knew were with the FBI.

She looked as disappointed as he felt while she cleaned her hands with the wet towelette next to her napkin. The prospect of her thinking with sadness about them parting pleased him.

She balled up the towelette and tossed it toward the ashtray. "Well, that was a little anticlimactic, wasn't it? The FBI, I mean. Here I thought I'd done something even I didn't know about."

Joe grimaced. He should have known she was thinking about the case.

She stared at him. "But why would they come into my room with their guns drawn?"

He shrugged. "They said they weren't entirely certain of your connection to Christine and thought it was a pretty good bet that she might be rooming with you."

"Oh."

He couldn't believe it. She was disappointed the FBI hadn't been after her. Go figure.

She scooted her chair back and got up. He quickly followed.

"Where to now?"

"Back to our old hotel, I guess. And to try to figure out what, exactly, is in that box that both Christine and the FBI are interested in."

# 10

RIPLEY SAT cross-legged on the bed in her original hotel room, the contents of the mysterious box spilled across the sheets in front of her. Hours of fingering the fake jewels, examining the clasps and the larger gems, holding them up to the lamplight and jingling them left her no closer to the truth than she'd been before.

She sighed and leaned back on her elbows, her gaze automatically drifting to the empty pillow beside her, then the wall her room shared with Joe's room.

When they'd returned to the hotel, she'd automatically assumed he would come to her room with her. But he hadn't. Instead he'd said something about contacting his home office and trying to work some sort of damage control and left her in her room, alone.

She straightened the watch on her wrist. That had been several hours ago. And he hadn't tried to contact her since.

She wasn't sure what she was supposed to think. Since the threat of the FBI wasn't hovering over them, and since Joe had already gotten her between the sheets, there was no longer a reason for them to be stuck together. She made a face, hating to describe their time together in that way. But it was accurate, wasn't it? She thought of his long, hard body and the many, many hours they had spent stuck together. Her stomach tightened with desire despite the dull sensation of feeling used that spread through her.

She dragged the free pillow over her head and groaned loudly, mostly because she couldn't quite bring herself to believe it had just been about the sex, no matter how phenomenal that had been. Joe had gone out on a limb for her in more ways than one. And people didn't do that for a roll in the hay.

But if he hadn't been with her merely for the sex, where was he?

She threw the pillow aside and sat up, pushing her hair from her eyes. She really shouldn't be thinking about that now. She should be trying to figure out what was in this box and why so many people were after it.

She picked up the box and fingered the semiprecious jewels dotting the side and lid. A soft knock on the door, and her intentions to solve the mystery flew straight out the balcony door.

She pulled the door open to find Joe standing there looking good enough to eat. "Hi," he said.

Gone were the jeans and casual shirt and back were the starched shirt, tie and dress slacks. She yanked on the tie, pulling him into the room. The door whooshed shut behind him.

He chuckled. "So you missed me, huh?"

She had. Bad.

"Here," he said, holding out a box to her. This one was a cardboard box similar to the ones that had littered the back seat of his car. "These are for you."

"You shouldn't have." She popped open the lid and stared at the athletic shoes inside. She fished one out and held it up. "Are we going somewhere?"

"I thought we might go for a walk."

"A walk." She considered him long and hard, then

her eyes widened in awareness. "Are you asking me for a date, Joe Pruitt?"

His immediate grimace spoke volumes.

"You are, aren't you?" she asked.

He cleared his throat, getting that ill-at-ease look again. He glanced at his watch. "I just got back from the company I'm trying to contract with and figured it was feeding time."

He glanced at the rumpled bed behind her, and Ripley waited for him to try to get her into it. Instead, he looked at her and asked, "Any luck with the box?"

She frowned and glanced at her shorts and shirt. There was no discernable difference that she could detect. But he had yet to make one suggestive remark or look at her breasts.

Not good.

"Okay. We'll go for a walk," she said carefully. "Just let me get dressed first."

JOE WALKED BESIDE RIPLEY, trying not to notice how well the red dress she'd changed into fit her, or how her breasts threatened to spill out of the top of it, making his mouth water for just a taste of the smooth, warm flesh. He swallowed hard, nodding at some lame comment she made on the history of Sun Studio and Elvis Presley.

Since she was obviously not going to wear the shoes he'd given her, he'd driven them to Beale Street, and instead of the walk he'd planned, they were walking the length of it. The sound of various blues bands filtered onto the street from the doorways they passed, the music sometimes slow and seductive, other times fast and lush. Even though the sun was sliding over the horizon, it was hotter than it had been at any other time of the day, a result of the asphalt beneath their feet having absorbed much of the sun's heat. Of course, Ripley's sexy attire wasn't helping in the heat area much, either, but Joe was trying not to notice that.

He sighed and wished he had changed into something more comfortable, cooler. He'd rolled his shirt sleeves to his elbows, loosened his tie and undid the first few buttons of his shirt, but he was sure he was sweating through the back of the crisp cotton.

A kid ran past them then launched into a series of flips the length of the sidewalk, then back again. Joe reached into his pocket, but Ripley caught his arm. "Let me."

She gave the preteen a couple of bills then tucked her hand easily into the crook of Joe's arm where he had stuffed his hands into his pockets. He felt his spine immediately snap straight and something akin to pride puff out his chest. She angled a smile at him, and he was sure she knew what had just happened. But rather than worry about her powers of observation, he merely smiled at her.

She lay her head briefly against his shoulder then lifted it. "So, tell me," she said quietly, "what's life like being Joe Pruitt?"

*Pretty damn dull*, he thought. At least until recently. He shrugged. "I don't know. The usual, I guess."

"Define the usual."

He squinted at her. "Are you hungry?"

"Not yet." She squeezed his arm through his shirt. "Since this was your idea, then you're going to have to start answering some of my questions."

"Define the usual," he repeated, slowing to allow another couple to pass in front of them. "I get up at six in the morning, go for a five-mile run if weather permits. In the office by eight. Out at five." He shrugged again. "The usual."

She hummed. "Except when you're traveling."

"Except when I'm traveling," he agreed.

"And how often do you do that?"

He made the necessary calculations. "Last year, I was on the road nearly thirty-two weeks."

"That much? That makes two-thirds of the time."

He nodded.

"So you travel as much as a rock star."

He chuckled. "Yes, as much as rock star. Just with different hours." And no groupies.

Trust Ripley to make his job sound more interesting than it was.

He caught himself. He'd never really thought of running his company as a job before. It was his career. His way of life. Never merely a job that he had to do to pay the bills.

"And you used to be a secretary," he said, unable to bring himself to compare her to Gloria. He couldn't imagine Ripley sitting still for more than five minutes at a time. Aside from the fact that she'd be damn distracting taking dictation.

Then again, if he had a secretary like Ripley, he probably wouldn't go out on the road as much as he did. He had four other low-level salesmen on the payroll who could take up much of the slack. But even when he'd hired them, he hadn't considered cutting back his travel hours.

"I was a secretary for six years," Ripley said quietly, as if the reality surprised her as much as him.

They walked in silence for another block, Ripley lingering in front of the glass fronts of nightclubs, watching the bands inside. Joe stared at his feet and felt pretty miserable, although he couldn't understand why.

When he'd left her alone at the hotel earlier, he'd decided to try to regain a hold on his life. He'd contacted Gloria and retrieved his messages and told her how he could be contacted. Then he put a call in to the company reps he had been wooing to set things in motion, only he didn't know how successful he'd been after an afternoon full of meetings he hadn't wanted to be in, his mind steadfastly on what kind of trouble Ripley was or wasn't getting herself into while he was away.

But he couldn't place the blame on her for his distracted state. Not completely, anyway. He was coming to realize that beyond his incurable lust for Ripley, and the bizarre, dreamlike quality of the past couple of days, what he was feeling for his job—it certainly wasn't an adventure—had been slowly lifting to the surface for the past few months. Landing distribution contracts, launching promotional campaigns and signing sports heroes to wear his products just weren't doing it for him anymore.

The problem was that beyond Ripley, he didn't know what *would* do it for him.

Then there was the little detail that soon not even Ripley would be in his life to distract him.

There was a tug on his arm. He looked to find her watching him curiously. "You know, I'm starting to worry about you," she said. "You haven't looked at my breasts once."

His gaze automatically drifted to the top of her dress and the soft, smooth skin there. "Yes, I have. You just haven't seen me do it."

Her smile was one hundred percent pure Ripley.

"Besides," he said. "I thought you hated that I had a one-track mind."

She seemed to consider his words. "One track is better than no track. Ever since this afternoon I feel like I've lost you."

*That makes two of us,* Joe thought.

Her hand slowly dropped to his, then she crossed in front of him, pulling him forward. "Tell me, what do you want to do? Name it. Anything, and we'll do it."

He wanted the world to start making sense again. But he didn't think that was going to happen anytime soon.

"Joe?"

"Hmm?" He blinked to stare into her face.

She stopped next to a lamppost, a decidedly suggestive smile curving her mouth. "Kiss me."

A groan started somewhere in the vicinity of his groin and twisted its way into his throat. Right that second, taking in her big brown eyes, pouty lips and suggestive expression, he couldn't name anything he'd rather do more.

Curving his fingers around her neck, feeling the throb of her pulse at the base, he slowly backed her against the lamppost, taking first one step, then another. Her eyes darkened as her gaze slid from his mouth to meet his gaze. Her tongue made a command performance, dragging across her full bottom lip, then dipping inside the slick depths of her mouth. Her back met with the post, and she reached to steady herself. Only Joe had no intention of allowing her to regain her equilibrium. He put his other hand on the pole above her head then bent and brushed his lips against hers.

Soft and sweet and heady. Joe closed his eyes and rested his forehead against hers, pulling his mouth mere millimeters away, their breath mingling between them. For an incredible moment, he wondered if he was going to survive her. And the question had nothing to do with the FBI, runaway clients or gun-pointing missing persons. Or even Ripley's penchant for finding trouble where none previously existed. No, his fear grew from knowing the woman herself. Watching her eyes brighten as she thought about her new career, the wrinkle between her eyebrows as she tried to figure out her case, her enthusiasm when she attacked a plate of ribs. He stroked his finger along her cheek and delicate jaw. There was also a lot to be said about the curve of her back as she strained against him during climax. The soft sounds she made when he thrust madly into her. The feel of her soft mouth covering his erection, giving him the complete attention she gave to everything else in her life.

Ripley stood staring at him, her whiskey-brown eyes full of questions. Then she tilted her mouth and pressed her lips more urgently against his.

Joe couldn't help but respond in kind.

The bustling street around them vanished, the world shrinking to include only Ripley where she stood in the pool of lamplight. As she dipped her tongue into his mouth, he couldn't help thinking she had crawled completely inside him over the past few days. He moved. He felt her right there under his skin even when they weren't together. His first waking thought was of her and where she was and how quickly he could sink into her silken, hot flesh. His last thought was to hold her to him as closely as possible to keep her from vanishing in the same mist that had brought her into his life.

The damnable part about the whole thing was that he didn't have a clue how she felt about him.

Ripley pulled away from the kiss, her soft, sexy laugh doing things to him that hands could never do. "Well, that was, um, nice."

He rolled an auburn curl between his fingers. "Nice?" he asked with a cocked brow.

"Very." She smiled then curled her hands into the open edges of his shirt. "Come on. I think we'd better go get something to eat before we get arrested for indecent exposure."

"We still have our clothes on."

"Exactly."

RIPLEY UNLOCKED the door to her room while still kissing Joe. In all honesty, she was afraid to stop kissing him for fear that he would get that serious expression on his face again and find an excuse to go to his own room. She pushed the door open with her hip, loving the taste of beer on his tongue, the feel of heat in his hands as he captured one of her breasts, pinching her tight nipple through the fabric of her dress. She let the strap of her purse slide off her shoulder, and the bag dropped to the floor with the weight of all it held.

Somehow she'd made it through dinner without diving straight into his lap and kissing that adorable but alarming expression from his face. She wished she knew what he was thinking, but she'd asked once, and he hadn't answered. She'd silently vowed not to hound him about it, too afraid she'd sound like her mother, who had a tendency to sound like a broken record when you weren't in a talking mood. Either that, or what you were thinking wasn't suitable to share with your mother.

She closed the door and pushed Joe against it, tugging his shirt from the waist of his slacks, then digging her fingers into the smooth, rippled flesh of his stomach. Maybe what Joe was thinking he couldn't share. While she didn't think he would lie to her about being married, it wasn't beyond the realm that he had a woman somewhere, a girlfriend maybe.

She didn't like the direction of her thoughts, so she stopped thinking altogether and concentrated on feeling.

And oh, boy, were there lots of feelings to be felt.

The instant they were in the privacy of her room, Joe thrust his hands up the short skirt of her dress, palming her bottom in that way that made her shiver with anticipation. Before she could get his shirt halfway unbuttoned, he'd stripped her of her panties. She gave up on the buttons and yanked the shirt off over his head, pressing her breasts against the solid wall of his chest. She sighed, loving the way he felt against her—her breasts smashed against his chest—his arousal hot and hard against her stomach.

He backed her toward the bed as he worked the zipper of her dress down. She tripped over something on the floor and he caught her, the incident affecting their mood not at all. They continued their blind search for the bed, and Ripley tripped over something else, this time something that sounded breakable. Her eyes flew open, and her mouth froze against Joe's.

"I hate to say it, but that doesn't sound good." He ground out the words between ragged gasps.

She agreed.

He kissed her hard again then reached to switch on the lamp. Only there was no lamp to be turned on.

"Wait here," he said.

Ripley groaned, reluctantly letting go of him so he could backtrack to the foyer and the switch there. Instantly, the room was awash in light. And Ripley didn't much like what she was seeing.

Joe let rip a string of ripe curses that Ripley wished she could have mouthed, if she were capable of speech at all.

The place was a mess. The lamp Joe had tried to turn on was the source of the glass sound. It lay on the floor, the bulb shattered, the bottom pulled off as if the something that someone had been looking for was inside the body of it. The mattress was slashed to shreds, pieces of stuffing and springs popping out at odd angles, and the pillows had been completely defeathered. Ripley hugged her arms around herself, noticing that not even her clothes had survived the search. Articles were strewn around the room. She picked up a T-shirt, eyeing the rip down the middle. She shivered, but this time it had nothing to do with Joe's hands on her bottom.

"I knew we should have gone to my room," he said under his breath.

AN HOUR LATER Ripley sat on the destroyed bed holding the card Agent Miller had given to Joe. There was nothing but a simple number printed in the middle. No name. Nothing to indicate if he or the other two men were, indeed, FBI.

After Joe had verified that his room had been left untouched, they'd called the hotel manager, who had called the police. They'd told the officials as much as they had to, considering that they didn't know much themselves. Joe was seeing the hotel manager out, assuring him that Ripley didn't need another room, that she would be staying with him but that that information wasn't for public knowledge. Should anyone call, hotel personnel were to say she had checked out.

Ripley cleared her throat. "Wait a minute."

Joe turned to face her from the door along with the manager.

"If anyone calls, I want them put straight through to Mr. Pruitt's room," she said.

Joe frowned at her.

She couldn't argue with him about staying in his room. The truth was, she didn't even want to contemplate sleeping alone tonight. Not when the person who had ripped her room apart had done such a thorough job of it. The police officers hadn't found the item used to rip apart the mattress, but they were fairly certain it had been a razor. Probably a straight edge, and a long one, at that.

Joe closed the door after the manager then came to sit on the destroyed bed next to her. She was grateful for the feel of his heat, although for an entirely different reason than before.

"What are you thinking?" he asked.

She glanced at him. "I don't know." She rolled everything around in her mind. Clarise Bennett, aka Christine Bowman. Nicole Bennett, whose name may or may not be Bennett at all. The FBI. The pawnshop....

Her heart did the equivalent of a tire skid across her chest.

"What is it?" Joe asked, watching as she got up and scrambled toward the door. She plucked up her purse then made her way to the bed. But rather than sitting again, she emptied the contents of her bag on the spread. She pushed aside her gun, her makeup bag, a pamphlet from the hotel, then found the item she wanted hiding under a wad of tissues.

The jewelry box.

"You had it with you?" Joe asked.

She nodded. "I stuck it into my bag right before we left, you know, thinking that if something occurred to me, I wanted to have it with me so I could go through it again."

She flipped the lid open and stared at the fake jewels inside.

Was it possible that they weren't fake? How much did the pawnshop owner really know about jewels? Could Nicole have told him they were fake, thinking they were, too, and he hadn't questioned it?

"So you know anything about jewelry?" she asked Joe.

He shook his head. "Not a thing."

"Me, either."

"You're not thinking what I think you're thinking, are you?"

"What, that they're real?"

"Yes."

"Then, yes, I am."

She crossed the room and picked up the phone, staring at the card still in her hand, then dialing the number there. "Only one surefire way to find out."

JOE STEPPED OUT of the shower, having finished in record time. "Ripley?" he called.

"What?" Her head popped into the doorway.

He grinned at her. "Nothing."

She rolled her eyes then walked into the other room.

Shortly after the phone call Ripley placed to Agent Miller to arrange for a meeting first thing in the morning, they'd gone to Joe's room. Not only was the security latch in place, he had moved a low bureau in front of the door, and he hoped like hell that Ripley would remain the only person ever to sneak into his bedroom via the balcony doors.

He hadn't wanted to leave her alone long enough to take a shower, but he'd been in dire need of one after their walk down Beale Street. He felt better now, not only because he'd had one, but because he was out again.

He draped a thick white towel around his hips and stepped into the other room where Ripley sat on the floor cross-legged, the box and its contents spread out, the television turned on low in front of her. ESPN? A girl after his own heart.

"Anything?" he asked.

She shook her head. "They still look fake to me."

He sat on the edge of the bed, drying his hair with another towel. "Maybe it's not the jewelry they were after."

She twisted her lips and looked at him. "What else could there be?"

He picked up the box. "The box itself, perhaps?"

He turned it around and around in his hands, looking inside, then out, then turning it upright. It didn't look like anything special to him. But what did he know?

"Wait," Ripley said softly, reaching to still his hands.

She positioned her head so she was staring under the box. Either that, or she was trying to sneak a peak under his towel. He was hoping it might be the latter. Unfortunately, it proved to be the former.

She steadied the box with one hand, then tugged on

something with another. He watched an orange-tabbed key drop to the floor.

"Oh, boy," Ripley whispered, plucking the key and holding it for him to see.

He turned the box over and stared at the fake bottom. Actually, it was more like a small compartment in the corner. Very easily missed, as both of them could attest to.

Ripley turned the key over in her hand.

"Looks like a locker key," Joe said. "One of those you find in an airport or something."

"Or a bus station, or a train station, or even a health spa."

He held his hand palm out, and she dropped the key into his palm. No identifying marks to indicate exactly where it was from, only the locker number, 401.

Ripley pulled her knees to her chest and rested her arms against them. "The locker could be anywhere from here to St. Louis and beyond."

He grimaced. "You weren't actually thinking to open it if you did know where it was, were you?"

She shrugged her slender shoulders. "Sure. The contents would probably help to explain a lot."

He reluctantly handed her the key then put the box on the bed next to him. "Judging by how things have gone down so far, I'd recommend against it."

She blinked at him. "And what would you recommend?"

"I say you should give the box and its contents to the FBI tomorrow, including the key."

She frowned, curling her toes against the carpeting. She had sexy toes. Slender, fingerlike, the nails painted a metallic pink. "Then we might never find out what's really going on."

"Fine by me."

Her brown eyes narrowed as she considered him. "Really? I mean, you can just walk away without knowing who Christine Bowman is, what Nicole's relationship is to her and what's in this locker to explain why the FBI's involved?"

"Walk away isn't the way I'd put it. Run would probably cover it more accurately."

She turned to stare at the key resting in the middle of her palm.

She just didn't get it, did she? He didn't care about Nicole Bennett, Christine Bowman or that damn key she held. All he cared about was her. And the only mystery he wanted to uncover was whether or not they had a future together.

# 11

RIPLEY SAT facing the three goons with FBI IDs who were squashed into the booth opposite her. She was concentrating on her breakfast. The middle goon elbowed the one on the end, and he nearly fell out of the bench and onto the floor, reminding her of an old Three Stooges episode.

The rejected agent stumbled to his feet, then stood, his mirrored sunglasses reflecting the table and its occupants but nothing about what was going on inside his head.

"Sir," a waitress said, trying to pass. "I'm going to have to ask you to sit down."

Not a flicker of emotion passed over his stone face as he gave their table a once-over, then moved to sit at the counter some fifteen feet away, positioning his stool so he could keep an eye on them.

"Where's the box?"

Ripley smothered jam on a half piece of toast. Ever since meeting in the lobby of the hotel half an hour ago, she'd been delaying giving the agents what they were after. There were a few things she wanted from them first. And she wasn't going to get what she wanted if she rolled over and played dead.

Okay, she'd had to concede to Joe that maybe trekking through every plane, train and bus station from Memphis to St. Louis wasn't a very good idea, even if she was chomping at the bit to see with her own two eyes what lay in the locker the key opened. So she'd offered a compromise. She'd hand the key over to her new friends here, but only when they shared some information with her.

She wiped her hands on her napkin then fished the box from her purse, the back of her hand grazing Joe's side where he sat beside her. His eyes held a mixture of amusement and exasperation.

"Here," she said, setting the box in the middle of the table.

Agent Miller glanced around the restaurant then plucked the box up while Ripley picked up her toast and took a bite.

A moment later, he stared at her. "Where's the rest?"

She squinted at him, pretending not to understand. "Can you take off your sunglasses, please? I don't much like talking to my own reflection."

He whipped them off so fast she was surprised he didn't put an eye out. He gave her a steely gaze that half tempted her to tell him to put the glasses back on. "Ms. Logan, I'd suggest you put your cards on the table now before I take you into protective custody and order a body search."

Obviously he'd used the threat before. And even she had to admit that the imagery wasn't particularly pleasant. "That would be a waste of time. It's not on me."

What went unsaid was that *it* was the key. The same key she'd sealed in an envelope and put in the hotel safe early that morning, long before the agents showed up for their meeting.

"Are you sure you don't want something to eat?" she asked.

They stared at her.

She shrugged and leisurely finished her breakfast, letting them chew on the information they already had—that she had the key and knew that they wanted it.

Joe shifted uncomfortably next to her. The waitress tried to refill his cup, and he put his hand over the rim to stop her. "Decaf, please."

Ripley accepted the full octane, then added four sugar packets and heavy cream. She looked Agent Miller full in the face. "I need you to fill in some missing gaps for me."

"What do you want to know?"

"What relationship does Nicole Bennett have to Christine Bowman, aka Clarise Bennett?"

For a long moment, it appeared he might not answer. Then finally he said in a short, clipped voice, "Bennett hired on as Bowman's housekeeper and cook a week ago."

Ripley raised her eyebrows. "Referred? Through an agency?"

"Cold interview as a result of an ad in a newspaper."

"Then she took off with the box."

"Yes."

"Which is why Christine followed Nicole here to Memphis."

He narrowed his eyes. Ripley shivered then stiffened her shoulders. "You've seen Christine Bowman?" the agent asked.

Joe leaned close to her. "I, um, left out the details of our little Clarise hunt the other night. Of course, I didn't know Clarise Bennett was Christine Bowman at the time, either."

God, but he smelled good. "Ah," she said slowly.

The agent leaned closer. "I need to know the details."

"Tell me what's in the locker first."

He went silent.

Ripley sighed, much as she would have had she been talking to a stubborn five-year-old. "Okay. But what I'm about to tell you I'm only offering as a good-faith gesture. With or without you, I am going to find out what's in the locker the key opens."

Silence again.

She launched into her explanation. "When we were making arrangements with the pawnshop owner to purchase the box and its contents, I noticed Christine getting out of a cab on the street outside. When I started to approach her she got back into the cab and took off. We followed her to the Pyramid, where we lost her. But we ran into an armed Nicole Bennett."

Agent Miller glanced at the agent next to him.

Ripley sighed. "I don't much like having my client run from me or having a gun held on me, so you can see why I'm interested in finding out what this is about."

Miller stared at her. "The pawnshop owner is dead."

Ripley nearly choked on her coffee.

Dead? The pawnshop owner was dead? She rested her head against her hands, trying to stop the spinning of the room. The problem lay in that the room wasn't spinning, she was.

"Define dead," Joe said quietly next to her.

Ripley looked up. Could Agent Miller have meant, "He's dead," as in, "I'm going to kill him for selling the box to you?" Figuratively speaking?

Miller motioned for the waitress to fill his cup when

she came with Joe's decaf. "His body was found late last night, stuffed inside one of his own display cases."

Nope, there was no figuratively in that equation.

Every last trace of bravado seeped from Ripley's muscles. She sank against the red plastic of the booth, wishing herself one with it. Images of her ransacked hotel room, her torn clothing, her shredded mattress chased the air from her lungs.

"Christine?" Joe asked.

The agent nodded. "We're guessing that right before she swung by your room with her straight edge, she made that visit to the pawnshop that she had aborted when you happened across her. I don't think she liked what the owner had to say. Clean shot straight to the head, execution style." He made a gun with his hand and pressed his index finger between his eyes. Ripley started when he made a *pow* sound.

"Oh, boy," she whispered, not for the first time feeling way out of her league here.

She'd never had direct contact with a known killer before. Clarise...Christine had seemed so normal. Just your average, everyday, run-of-the-mill woman concerned about her sister's welfare.

"Who *is* this person?" she asked.

"If we told you, we'd have to kill you."

Ripley nearly dropped her coffee cup. He cracked a small smile.

"Ha, ha. Agent humor. I get it."

The smile disappeared. "The only thing you need to know is that she's a dangerous woman. We've been trailing her for over ten months now, trying to get the drop on her, and she's always been one step ahead of us."

"Until Nicole, who I'm guessing is a thief, unwittingly targeted Christine's house."

"Right."

"Do you know where the locker is?" Joe asked.

The agent didn't blink, didn't say anything.

Ripley swallowed. "I'll take that as a yes."

"Ms. Logan, I can't emphasize enough how important it is that you give us that key. So long as you have it, you remain a target."

"A target for what?"

He really didn't have to answer that, and thankfully he didn't.

Joe slid his arm around the back of the booth then pulled her to rest against his side. She was glad for his closeness and warmth. Suddenly, she felt cold.

"Explain something. How does your gaining possession of the key help me?" she asked. "As far as you know, Christine doesn't know of your involvement. So if I hand over to you what she wants, then she's going to think I still have it anyway."

"She already suspects we're onto her."

"Maybe so, but how does she know I handed over the key? Unless..."

"Unless you tell her that," Joe finished for her.

Ripley sat bolt straight. "Call me stupid, but I'd prefer it if I didn't have to come within spitting distance of Christine Bowman again, at least not in this lifetime."

Everyone at the table went eerily silent. Ripley stared at the empty plates that had held her super breakfast, wondering if it had been a mistake to eat all she had. Of course, when she'd thought she'd get one over on the agents, she hadn't known murder was included anywhere in the picture. The waitress cleared her plates away, and she was left with nothing to stare at but the other men at the table. After flicking a gaze at the two agents across from her, she looked at Joe, and felt sanity slowly return.

So Nicole Bennett was a thief who had cased and targeted Christine Bowman's house, stealing from someone who was already on the wrong side of the law, eliminating any risk of Christine reporting the theft to the police. She'd brought the goods to Memphis, unloaded them at the pawnshop and...

But that didn't explain why she didn't leave after the sale. Why had she been at the Pyramid?

Ripley shook her head. Wrong avenue. This wasn't about Nicole, it was about Christine.

Then it occurred to her. A plan that would take care of Christine, keep her and Joe safe and, she hoped, give her the answers she was looking for.

"Tell me what's in the locker, and I'll tell you how we're going to handle this," she said stoically.

JOE WAS RUNNING on borrowed time. He'd pretty much figured that out over breakfast with Ripley and the three agents. Hell, he'd worked out that much one day into his bizarre, sexy relationship with her. But now that their plane had touched down in St. Louis, and he and Ripley were in her ancient Ford Mustang—which might have been a classic had the previous owner or owners taken care of it—chugging toward her apartment, he could hear the clock ticking on the time he had left with Ripley.

"Diamonds," Ripley whispered next to him, kicking the windshield wipers into action to combat the rapidly falling rain.

Heavy gray clouds choked the sky, seeming to crowd around the car as she negotiated the slippery streets to her place. It was just after noon, but the storm overhead made it look more like dusk. There was a burst of lightning on the horizon, then a crack of thunder seemed to shake the already shaky vehicle. What Joe wouldn't do for his own car, which was sitting in a parking lot at Memphis International Airport.

Diamonds. That's what Agent Miller had finally told Ripley was in the storage locker. Ten months ago someone hit a wholesale jeweler in New York, making off with a bag of flawless, uncut white diamonds. That person was Christine Bowman. The catch was that they hadn't had much luck in proving the priceless gems were in Christine's custody, thus the reason she had yet to be arrested. Then Nicole Bennett had entered the picture and had thrown everything into a tailspin.

That connection between Christine and the diamonds was what Ripley had promised to give the agents.

"Do you think they told us the truth?" Ripley asked him, taking her eyes from the road.

"Whoa," he said, grabbing the dashboard. "Can we talk about this when we get to your place?" *And off this slippery road in this poor excuse for a car.*

She waved off his comment. "I drive in this stuff all the time. Have to, or else I'd be housebound now, wouldn't I? Besides, we're not going to my place. Not yet." She looked directly at him. "Anyway, I'm still waiting for an answer to my question."

"I'd feel better if this old thing had a passenger-side air bag." He glanced at her. "And what do you mean we're not going to your place?"

She smiled.

He released a long breath. "Why wouldn't they tell you the truth?"

"I don't know. Call me cynical, but everything connected with this case hasn't been what it seems."

Everything? Joe looked at her, wondering if that comment extended to them and their tentative relationship.

He ran a hand through his damp hair. "Back to the not going to your place part..."

The plan Ripley had worked out with Miller included her returning to St. Louis, going straight to her apartment and waiting for Christine Bowman to contact her. The minute she did, Ripley was to arrange for a public meeting in which she would ask for what remained on her fee and then pass the box, including the key, to Christine. Pretend she'd never been contacted by the FBI. That she didn't know Christine was indeed Christine. And act like she had no idea the pawnshop owner had been stuffed in his own display case. Ripley was a simple P.I. who had performed a simple task. She'd tracked down Nicole, recovered the stolen items her client directed her to, and was returning those items. Nothing more, nothing less.

And Joe liked absolutely nothing about this.

He glanced over his shoulder at the road behind them. He was pretty sure that agents were tailing them, but he'd be damned if he could make them out. "You know, they're not going to like this very much."

"Tough." She glanced at him. "Besides, where I'm going will only take a few minutes."

"And that is?"

"The park."

"Hmm. The park." The response should have surprised him, but it didn't. Only Ripley knew how Ripley's mind worked. Like always, he was just along for the ride.

She rubbed her palms over the steering wheel. "You see, while we know what the locker holds, we still don't know its location."

"And that affects us how?"

She looked at him. "I want to be there when Christine goes after those diamonds."

Joe stared at it her. Had she gone completely insane? Forget that they were talking about a woman who didn't hesitate to whack those who didn't cooperate with her. There was no telling what she would do if she spotted Ripley anywhere within a hundred-mile radius of that locker.

"I think it's safe to assume it's here in St. Louis," she said, appearing to think aloud. "Miller would never have asked us to return here if it weren't. Besides, this is where Christine started out. The only reason we ended up in Memphis in the first place was—"

"Because of Nicole Bennett."

Joe didn't know what concerned him more. That he was in tune enough with her to finish her sentences or that he was nodding in agreement.

He cleared his throat. "So how do you propose we find out where this locker is?" He glanced out the back window again. "I think our friends will be suspicious if we start hitting bus and train stations." He jabbed a thumb toward the back seat. "And we just left the airport and didn't check there."

"How?" Her smile made something go thump in his chest. "You'll see."

"I was afraid you were going to say that."

A few minutes later Joe pretty much thought he had their tail pegged. It was a late model SUV with a woman driving, though there was a baby seat in the back—empty—and the guy wearing a ball cap in the passenger's seat appeared somehow too relaxed. But when Joe suspected Ripley didn't make an expected turn, the guy sat up, instantly alert.

He glanced at Ripley. God, but even now he found her the most attractive woman he'd ever been around. It was more than physical beauty. A buzzing kind of energy seemed to emanate from her, a thirst for life that made him hum just being next to her. Made him question things he wasn't so sure he wanted to question. Made him want her beyond anything having to do with sex. Well, okay, sex, too. But he was increasingly wanting more, while she appeared happy with the way things were.

She pulled to the side of the road and parked at the curb, throwing the car into park. She glanced at him, the telltale way she worried her bottom lip making his stomach tighten. "Um, I think it would be a good idea, you know, if you waited here."

"Not a chance in hell."

She grabbed his arm when he moved to climb out.

"Please, Joe."

A great pair of breasts and pleading. A lethal combination. And two things he could never resist. At least not in Ripley.

"Fine," he said, feeling anything but fine.

He watched her get out of the car and visually followed her form as she walked toward the park. The SUV slowly passed, and Joe watched it, wanting to throw his hands in the air in exasperation.

BY THE TIME Ripley pulled up next to the park located on the banks of the Mississippi, the Arch visible just over the rise, it had stopped raining. Although judging from Joe's stormy expression, she was surprised it hadn't started pouring *inside* the car.

Unfortunately, she didn't think his countenance was going to change anytime soon.

Not many knew of her friendship with Nelson Polk beyond the boundaries of the park. She didn't think her mother would be very happy if Ripley brought him home to dinner, although she had thought about inviting him a couple of times. She'd settled, instead, for buying him a bite or two or three at a nearby diner. It wasn't that she was ashamed of him, exactly. She knew others might not understand her bond with this fifty-something washed-up private investigator for whom a bottle of cheap red wine comprised his entire food intake.

And it looked like he'd had a little too much to eat today.

"Nelson, I need a favor from you." A big favor. A humongous favor. Although she was afraid it was going to take an act of God to get anything from the man slumped in his chair, his chess set closed on the table in front of him, his mouth hanging open in mid-snore.

Ripley glanced uneasily toward her car some hundred yards away, a car for which she'd traded in her two-year-old Taurus with three years of payments left in order to lower her overhead. She moved so she blocked Joe's view of Nelson, then crouched next to her friend.

"Oh, please, don't do this to me now, Nelson," she whispered, closing her eyes.

At that moment it was hard to recognize the sloshed, barely conscious man next to her as the guy who shared so many words of wisdom over a competitive game of chess. She'd never seen him this far gone and wondered what had caused him to drink himself into such a state. She reached out and rested her warm hand over his cold one.

"Ripley? Is that you?" he slurred, without opening his eyes.

Her heart did a little drumbeat. "Yes, Nelson, it is."

He smiled, making his two-day-old gray stubble stick out all the more. "Thought so."

"Nelson...I need your help."

The smile vanished. "Help. A lot of people asking for help these days. Unfortunately it seems to be in short supply."

Ripley squinted at him, wondering who else had asked him for help, and in what form it had come. "Actually, I think this kind of help is right up your alley." She looked toward the churning waters of the Mississippi, then at the sky, which looked moments away from opening up again. But Nelson was dry. Either he had just made his way to the park bench or the tree overhead had protected him from the worst of the previous downpour. "You remember when I told you about that first case I took on?"

His eyelids cracked open, and brown eyes peered at her. "Uh-huh."

She smiled overly brightly. "Well, guess who needs some information and you're the only guy she can get it from?"

He didn't say anything for a long moment. But his eyes remained semiopen, and he appeared to be considering her long and hard. Either that or he could sleep with his eyes open. "So," he said finally, making her jump, "that's why you haven't been to see me lately. This case."

"I've been in Memphis."

He struggled to sit up, only whatever he'd drunk wasn't cooperating.

"Nelson, how about I treat you to some coffee?"

He grinned at her. "I'd love a cup."

"NELSON, I'm sorry to say this, but I think you're going to be spending the next two days in the bathroom," Ripley said, stepping to the diner table with two extra-large cups of coffee. She slid them in front of the tattered old man, then slid into the booth next to Joe.

This was the guy who had inspired Ripley to become a private investigator? Joe stared, astounded, at Nelson's gnarled hands as he pushed aside the cup he'd just drained then reached for one of the others. He rubbed the back of his neck and glanced out the window, where the SUV was stopped across the street, the agents inside pretending to consult a map.

That's what Joe could use right about now—a map to find his way out of the mess he was sitting in the middle of.

"How are you feeling?" Ripley asked.

Joe glanced at her, but she hadn't directed the question to him. Instead, she was gazing at Nelson Polk as if he was Moses, seeming unaffected by the ripe smell coming from him and his unwashed clothes.

Polk nodded. "Better." He turned unfocused eyes on her. "At least now I know that I'm not seeing double, and the guy next to you must be a friend."

Ripley smiled. "Nelson, this is Joe Pruitt. He's a shoe salesman."

Nelson's bushy white brows moved upward on his ruddy face. "A shoe salesman. A respectable position."

"I suppose you could say that." Joe grimaced, not up to correcting the description. He was a whole hell of a

lot more than a shoe salesman. Well, at least he was before he met one sexy, insane Ripley Logan.

Nelson quickly drained the second cup of coffee, obviously familiar with the routine. Color began returning to his face, and he sat a little straighter in the booth.

"So tell me about your case, Rip," he asked even as
he popped the lid off the third cup, this time adding a
good portion of sugar and cream to it before bringing it
to his lips.

Ripley told him, from first being hired by Clarise
Bennett—information Joe suspected Polk already
knew—then finding out she was really Christine Bowman, to where they were sitting across from the old
man in the diner.

Joe glanced at his watch. All within five minutes.
And if he didn't know better, he'd say that Polk had
not only followed every word of the explanation, but
understood them. Which put him way ahead of Joe. Joe
still wasn't convinced he understood what was going
on.

"Where's the key?" Polk asked.

Ripley glanced toward the window and the SUV
parked on the opposite side of the street. She reached
into the pocket of her jeans, palming the key, then
holding her hand palm down for Polk to take.

"Be careful that our friends don't see what you're
doing," she said.

"I wondered whose friends they were. For a minute
I was afraid they were mine," Polk said, adding pocket
change to his hand then cupping it and pretending to
be counting out the price of the coffees. "Got yourself
in mighty deep first case out of the gate, didn't you?"
The smile he gave her was affectionate, and now that
he no longer looked like he was going to fall face first to

the tile and start snoring, Joe noticed he appeared shrewd.

Great, that's all they needed. A homeless Colombo.

Polk held his hand out to Ripley, dumping the contents into it. It didn't appear he'd glanced at the key long enough to make a determination. Joe fully expected him to say he didn't have a clue.

"The bus station."

Joe blinked.

"The bus station? Are you sure?"

"Positive." Polk sipped leisurely at his coffee. "Which makes sense considering the traffic around there lately."

"What traffic?" Joe found himself asking.

Ripley and Polk stared at him. He shrugged, acting like he'd been involved in the conversation from the onset.

Polk subtly motioned toward the window. "More of your friends hanging around there. Brooklyn Bob was complaining about the lack of prime bench space there this morning. They've had the place under surveillance for at least the past month, but traffic picked up considerably over the past couple of days."

Ripley leaned across the table and gave Polk a sound kiss on the cheek. Joe cringed. Polk beamed.

"You're a prince among men, Nelson."

No comment, Joe thought.

# 12

TWENTY MINUTES and a meal fit for a prince later, Joe watched Ripley pull up to a curb on a downtown street and maneuver her way into a spot that didn't appear large enough to hold a golf cart. Amazingly she squeezed into it without incident, while the driver of the SUV drove past them as if she hadn't a care in the world. And, Joe guessed, she probably didn't. Additional agents were probably already set up around the area to keep an eye out for Ripley and to throw off anyone else who might be watching her.

"You ready?" she asked, grabbing an old newspaper from the back seat and spreading it, presumably to shield her head from the pounding rain that had picked up again after they left the diner.

Ready? Hell no, he wasn't ready. But the alternative was sitting in the car alone for an unspecified amount of time. He watched her get out of the car and run around it toward the sidewalk to his right. He opened the door and sprinted after her.

The building was an older brick construction, four stories high, four apartments to each floor. The wet paper plastered to her head, Ripley unlocked the outer door, then quickly ushered him inside. Another key and they had access to the hall and the stairs.

She peeled the paper from the side of her face and offered a sheepish smile. "I used to have a nice place in a newer subdivision in the suburbs, but I thought an apartment downtown could serve double duty as an office. You know, until I can afford to rent commercial space."

She was apologizing for where she lived, he realized. "I've lived in worse places," he said.

She looked at him skeptically.

"Okay, no, I haven't. But I don't see anything wrong with this place."

"You haven't seen the apartment yet."

He didn't say anything as she led the way up the stairs. And up. And up again. Now he knew how she kept that tidy little figure despite how much she put away at the dinner table. She stepped to the first door to the right and opened it, flipping a switch just inside. She stood aside for him to enter.

SOMEHOW the tiny apartment seemed even smaller with Joe Pruitt's huge frame standing in the middle of the combination living and dining area. Ripley watched his face for his reaction, then looked around the place herself. The furniture wasn't bad. She'd bought it all when she'd had a nice condo just outside the city, so she wasn't concerned about that. It was the water stains on the ceiling that no amount of repainting had been able to get rid of. The chipped sink visible in the small kitchen off to the left. The scarred floor that had been under the green shag carpeting she had pulled up her first day in the apartment, thinking anything had to be better than the rug. She'd been right, but just barely. And her area rugs didn't nearly cover the surface.

She put her hands on his shoulders. He started then turned to stare at her. She gave a nervous laugh.

"Looks like we're going to be here for a while. I, um, thought maybe you'd like to take your jacket off until then, especially since it's dripping on my floor."

"Oh." He shrugged out of his suit jacket. She shook it on the rug near the door then draped it over the radiator in the dining room. The top of the one in the living area was filled to overflowing with plants meant to cover it.

A punch to her answering machine revealed three messages. The first two were from her mother, inviting her to dinner. The last one was nothing but air. The machine said it was left a half hour ago. She shivered, then stepped to the front window where she'd closed the curtains before she'd left for Memphis. She peeked from the side, staring at the street below.

The plan was that she would come to her apartment with the hope that Christine Bowman would contact her here in search of the key. Of course, Ripley wasn't supposed to let on that she even knew of its existence. Instead, when Christine made contact, Ripley would give her the entire box.

"Are they out there?" Joe whispered.

His breath disturbed the damp hair near her ear, making her shiver. He was referring to the FBI, who had promised to have someone watching her, just in case Christine decided to do to her what she'd done to her mattress last night. Agent Miller had offered to have one of his agents trade places with Joe as an extra precaution. Ripley had passed, feeling far safer with Joe than she would with a hundred agents.

"I don't see anyone."

She remained at the window, though her sight had turned inward, her every nerve ending aware of where Joe stood so close yet not touching her.

Last night after the break-in, she'd crawled into his bed, expecting him to follow her, to take up where they'd left off before she'd nearly tripped over the broken lamp in her room. But he hadn't joined her. Instead, she'd jerked awake at some point during the night to find him sleeping at an awkward angle on the couch, his position allowing him a view of the room door, the balcony doors and the bed. The big lug had been protecting her. The least she could do was get him a pillow and a blanket. And she had, even though she'd mostly wanted to wake him and drag him into bed with her.

Since then he'd been...distant somehow. Preoccupied. He'd barely said a word to her on the plane ride home. Then again, she'd been so consumed with what she'd learned that morning, creeped out by the knowledge that the pawnshop owner had been killed, that she probably hadn't been very good company herself. In fact, she knew she hadn't.

"What if she pulls a gun on me?" she murmured, referring to Christine.

Finally she felt him touch her...of all places, on her feet.

Positioning his shoulder to balance her, he lifted first one leg, then the other, slipping off her shoes and massaging the pads of her feet. She moaned, thinking that this was definitely something she could get used to, this thing Joe had for her feet.

In fact, Joe was something she could find herself getting used to. No matter where they were or what was happening, all he had to do was touch her, and every last thought vanished from her head, leaving her with nothing but longing.

He put her right foot on the floor then stood so he

was behind her. His hand curved around her waist then came to rest against her stomach. A small tug left her back flush with his front. "I'll be there, right alongside you."

She covered his hand with hers, reveling in the feel of him against her. "Somehow the thought of you buying it along with me isn't very reassuring, but thanks anyway."

He skimmed his lips over her right ear. "Well, then, we'll have to make sure she never gets a chance to squeeze off a shot, won't we?"

And that was the plan. If Christine called, Ripley was going to give her directions to her apartment...if she didn't already know the way. Ripley would instruct Christine to slip the recovery fee into her mailbox downstairs, then exit the building to stand on the sidewalk across the street where Ripley could see her. Ripley would retrieve the money and put the box between the two security doors, propping open the outer door before hightailing it up the steps to safety.

The click of her thick swallow sounded awfully loud in the quiet apartment.

"Nervous?" Joe asked.

She nodded.

"Good. That means you are human, after all."

She turned in his arms, bringing her chest-to-chest with him. The brushing of her erect nipples against his hard chest nearly made her forget what she was going to say. "I don't know if this is such a good idea. Maybe we should change the meeting place to somewhere public."

His gaze swept over her face. "You *are* scared."

She glued herself more tightly to him, resting her cheek against his shoulder and squeezing her arms around him so hard she was pretty sure he was having difficulty breathing.

His hands hesitated on her back, then slid up and down, cupping her bottom in his palms and pressing her against him. "You know, there are things we could do to keep ourselves occupied until she calls."

She smiled against his shoulder. "Yes, that there are."

Only she wasn't sure she would be such good company. Her mind was so packed full of information it felt like it might explode. And her nerves were stretched to the breaking point.

One of Joe's hands slipped between them and fit around her breast. She caught her breath, amazed by how quickly every last bit of that information zapped from her head and how loudly her nerves started clamoring for the release they knew he could give her.

She hugged him tighter, trapping his hand between them. She honestly didn't know what she would have done if she hadn't made the mistake of crawling into bed with him on that fateful night. He made her laugh, sometimes want to scream in exasperation, more often cry out in such exquisite passion that she had begun not to recognize herself in the mirror. A transformation begun when she'd switched professions but completed when she invited Joe Pruitt between her thighs. He awakened emotions in her she couldn't begin to identify. Emotions that demanded merely to be felt, rather than analyzed. Lived and breathed rather than denied.

"Thank you for this," she whispered, rubbing her cheek against the crisp cotton of his shirt.

"For what?"

She pulled back to look into his overwhelmingly handsome face. "Oh, I don't know. For not saying anything when I hopped into your bed, maybe. Or for not bolting in the other direction even when you were sure I didn't have a clue about what I was doing." Her gaze dropped to his mouth. His hot, generous mouth. "For, um, coming back here with me when it would have been easier for you to leave me at the Memphis airport."

"You act like I had a choice," he murmured.

She tried to step away, but he wouldn't allow her the freedom.

"You don't understand what I mean by that, do you?"

She stared at him, spellbound, afraid to ask for fear he might say she'd railroaded him into coming along.

He freed the hand trapped between them and ran his fingers through her hair, pulling it back and holding it there. "You have no idea how I feel about you, do you, Ripley Logan?"

She blinked. She felt evidence of how he felt growing thick and hard between them. She pressed her hips into his and smiled. "Oh, I think I have an idea."

His eyes darkened, but she wasn't convinced desire was completely to blame. "I don't think you do."

His gaze flitted to her lips, her ear, her hair where he held it, then to her eyes. "Sure, I'll be the first to admit that when you popped into my bed that night, all that was on my mind was sex." He smiled faintly. "I am only human, you know." His fingers lowered to rest at the base of her neck. "Then I got to know you. Spent some time with you. You asked me questions I would never have dared ask myself. Made me take a closer look at my life, at what I was doing with it. Or, rather, what I wasn't doing with it."

"Joe, I—"

"Shh." He pressed his fingers against her lips, appearing to have a difficult time not kissing her. "I'm trying to be serious here."

"That's what's scaring me," she whispered.

He frowned at her.

She dropped her gaze to his chest, pretending a phenomenal interest in the whiteness of his shirt. "There's so much going on now…happening… Joe, I don't know which end's up."

He stared at her long and hard. "Then I think I should show you."

He launched an all-out assault on her mouth that left her knees buckling under her and her body screaming in sheer pleasure. Even as her mind called out, *no, no!* her limbs melted against his and her heart countered with an even louder, *yes, yes!* His erection pressed hard and insistent against her stomach, and a need to have it pressing inside of her, pushing everything else from her mind, overwhelmed her. Her fingers were in his hair, on his chest, over his tight rear, as her mouth fought to keep up with his.

"Where's the bedroom?" he asked, his hand up her blouse and under her bra and stroking her nipple to aching hardness.

She licked her lips, then kissed him again. "Behind you. To your left."

She fumbled for his belt, pulling it loose as he backed them toward the closed bedroom door.

Closed…

The word rang in her passion-filled mind, but she couldn't seem to grasp the importance of it. Not when there were other more pressing needs clamoring for attention.

Joe reached for the handle and opened the door, and

she reached for his zipper, then an ominous metallic click told them they weren't alone.

RIPLEY HAD NEVER felt so violated, so helpless. Just a short while ago she'd been questioning the wisdom of arranging a meeting at her apartment for the simple reason that she wasn't comfortable with Christine Bowman knowing where she lived. Suppose something went wrong? Suppose the FBI didn't catch Christine with the diamonds red-handed and she got away? Suppose she blamed Ripley for the close call and came back looking for revenge?

Of course as Ripley sat with her hands tied behind her back, Joe sitting next to her, none of that made a bit of difference. Christine had been in her apartment all along, waiting for them, probably even before their plane had touched down at Lambert Airport.

They should have come up with a way to alert the FBI when they were in trouble. Another moot point because Ripley couldn't have moved if she'd tried.

Seeming satisfied with her handiwork, Christine pulled a dining room chair out and sat down, looking at them where she'd tied them up on the tiny kitchen floor. Heat seemed to radiate from Joe. She glanced to find his jaw flexing angrily, his eyes steadfastly on Christine. She nudged his leg with hers. Anger wouldn't get them anywhere but dead.

"Where's the box?" Christine asked, looking directly at Ripley.

The other woman wore black leather pants, a black Lycra tank top and black leather gloves. Her blond hair was pulled into a twist, and the gun looked right at home in her hands.

Why hadn't Ripley noticed what a con artist she was

when they first met? It could have been the plain flow-ered dress. The fluffy blond hair that looked like she'd just come from the hairdressers. Her horror at having nicked a nail while hiring Ripley.

Now she looked like she could play the starring role in a vampire flick, right down to her blood-red lipstick.

Ripley purposely cleared her throat. "Clarise, what are you doing? I don't understand—"

"Cut the crap, Logan," Christine said, sighing. "I know you're on to me. I also know about your new lit-tle friends sitting outside your apartment right now."

Interesting how everyone kept referring to the FBI as her friends when they were anything but. Any law en-forcement friends worth their salt would never have let this woman gain access to her apartment.

"You know, if you hadn't run from us outside the pawnshop, we probably never would have figured it out," Joe said.

"Then there's the little matter of your phone being disconnected," Ripley added.

Christine lifted a finely penciled brow. "Who are you kidding? Neither of you would have figured out anything if not for the Feds." She cocked the gun, a 9mm similar to Ripley's, except in gunmetal black. "The box."

Ripley had never wanted to hit, really hit, anyone before. But oh, boy, did she want to sock it right to Christine Bowman in her red-painted mouth.

Then she remembered that the box didn't hold the key Christine was looking for. The key was in Ripley's back pocket.

"Over there," Ripley said. "In the bag near the door."

Christine stared at her for a long moment.

"What?" Ripley asked. "I'm tied up, remember?"

Christine pushed from the chair, trying to keep them in sight as she went to the door and rifled through Ripley's duffel. Unfortunately for her, and fortunately for Ripley, Christine had picked the one blind spot in the apartment to tie them up.

Awkwardly maneuvering her hands, Ripley slid the locker key out of her back pocket and began working the jagged edge against the thin rope that bound her wrists together. She winced when the rope cut into her flesh.

"What are you doing?" Joe whispered harshly.

She glanced at him, then at Christine, who had her back to them trying to find the box, which Ripley had wound in clothing and tucked way at the bottom of the bag for safekeeping.

"Shh." She hushed him.

The damn key wasn't accomplishing anything. But her movements trying to saw the rope had. Somehow she'd managed to work the ropes a little looser. She winced as the binding cut into her wrists again. There. All she had to do—

Christine found the box.

Ripley urgently leaned over and slid the key into Joe's front pants pocket. He stared at her.

"The key." Christine appeared in the kitchen doorway, such as it was, the gun at her side, her expression clearly exasperated.

"You know, when I picked your name out of the paper, I really never saw you getting this far." She smiled, her teeth white against her red lips. "No, the other two overpaid idiots were the ones who were supposed to get the job done. But surprise of surprises, you're the one who came through. Good thing I'm a woman who likes to cover her bases, isn't it?''

Ripley didn't know if she should feel complimented or insulted. She decided on insulted.

"The key," she repeated.

"In my pocket," Joe said. "The left one."

Ripley glanced at him, not missing the message he was trying to send her not to do anything.

Christine stood stock-still, then motioned for Joe to scoot forward. He did. She reached into his pocket and took out the key, then waved her gun for him to back up.

The grin that spread across her face would have been attractive, if only Ripley didn't know she was a murderer. "Bingo."

Ripley swallowed hard. "What about my fee?"

Christine stared at her as if she were speaking a foreign language.

"You still owe me money, whether you're Christine or Clarise," Ripley said. "Do you have any idea how much I lost tracking down that box?"

Christine laughed so hard she nearly dropped her gun. Nearly, but unfortunately not quite.

"Oh, you're priceless." She tossed the key in the air then caught it. "But not nearly worth as much as what's in this locker."

Ripley opened her mouth to say something when Christine cocked the 9mm and stepped forward to settle the muzzle against Ripley's forehead. The strangled cry that filled the kitchen very definitely came from her throat.

Joe jerked next to her. "You got what you wanted." He ground out the words. "Now why don't you just get the fuck out of here?"

Christine glanced at him.

"We're tied up. Just what do you think we're going to do? Scoot on our asses and follow you?"

She appeared to consider that as Ripley stared beyond the barrel of the gun, the metal cold against her skin. A crazy prayer wound around and around her mind. *Please, please don't let her shoot me and get gray matter all over Joe's nice white shirt.*

Christine stepped back, taking her gun with her. Ripley nearly dissolved into a puddle of relief at her feet.

"You're right," Christine said. "I'll be long gone before either one of you has the chance to tell anyone what went down here." She smiled. "Besides, I suppose I do owe Ripley, here, for getting back my property."

"Does that mean I'm going to get paid?"

Not even Ripley could believe she'd uttered the words as Christine and Joe stared at her.

"You know, in another lifetime, you and I might have been friends." Christine laughed, then turned and was gone, the apartment door clicking closed behind her.

Ripley refused to give in to the incredible desire to close her eyes and instead tried to come to terms with all that had just happened. It wasn't every day someone held a gun to your head, threatening to kill you for a job you did right. Of course, she didn't think very many people got that type of reaction for messing up, either, but that was neither here nor there.

Instead, she scrambled to her knees as she shrugged her way out of her bindings. In no time flat she had Joe freed, as well. She scrambled to the phone and called the number Miller had given her.

"She's got the key. Christine Bowman's got the key."

# 13

JOE DIDN'T LIKE THIS. Everything felt...wrong.

"Come on," Ripley said, getting out of her Mustang and running across the street, her raincoat blowing behind her like a cape. Joe shook his head, not liking the superhero imagery that came to mind at the vision.

Of course, it didn't help matters that he hadn't been able to get down a decent swallow since Christine Bowman had stood with that damn gun pressed against Ripley's flawless forehead. Within a blink of an eye, it seemed that everything important to him was about to be taken away. Both the realization that Ripley had grown to be so important to him and the fear that he'd never get to tell her that was enough to knock any guy's legs out from under him.

Add to that Ripley's need to go to the bus station to see Christine's capture, despite what had happened at her apartment, and he was operating solely on autopilot. Half of him wanted to pin her down with his body weight and make her admit what she felt for him was more than sexual, while the other half was filled with the desire to tie her up again and leave her to sit in her apartment, alone, until all this was over with.

The rain came down in a torrent, an all-out summer shower that turned dusk to midnight. He rushed after Ripley across the street and to the bus station entrance, earning himself a honk from a driver coming from his left.

How did you like that for discreet?

The instant Ripley had placed the call to Miller, they'd watched through her apartment window as two cars pulled from parked positions on either side of the street and roared away, obviously positioning themselves for Christine's arrest. Of course, had they been doing their jobs right, Christine would never have gotten into Ripley's apartment in the first place. But right now, that was neither here nor there, was it?

Ripley ducked to the side of the bus station door. Joe sidled up next to her, uncomfortable in the T-shirt she'd given him to wear—something purple with a picture of Winnie the Pooh on it, and a Cardinals ball cap—while she wore a floppy beige rain cap that covered the hair she'd tied into a knot on top of her head, and a trench coat that made her look like the detective she was.

"You know, we could both just go back to your place, order up some pizza and read about this in tomorrow's paper," he said.

She gave him a long-suffering look and led the way inside. Well, he thought, it was worth one last try, anyway.

They paused just inside the door. The station was bustling with the traffic Polk had told them about. Joe kept his head down as he scanned the stark interior of the station. In fact, Polk himself had taken up residence on one of the benches, a brief wink all the acknowledgment he gave Ripley.

"I knew he wouldn't be able to pass this one up," she said to Joe, yanking her collar up.

"What in the hell are you doing here?"

A homeless man had come up behind them. Joe eyed him, noticing he didn't smell the way Polk did. Then he realized it wasn't a homeless man at all, but Agent Miller. He glanced around them, then held his hand out and asked for a dollar for a cup of coffee, speaking with a slurred voice slightly louder than the one he'd first addressed them with.

Joe began digging in his pockets as Ripley looked around.

"I want...no, I'm ordering you to turn around and go right back out the way you came in," Miller fairly growled. "Bowman spots you, this is all over with before it starts."

Joe looked at Ripley hopefully. Pizza and her were sounding mighty good right about now.

"No way," she whispered harshly, that stubborn look on her face. "I'm in this till the end."

"End being the operative word, Ms. Logan," Miller said. "Look, I don't know how in the hell you found out where the locker was—" Ripley flashed him a smile "—but I want you out of here. Now. If you don't leave willingly, I'll see to it that a couple of men will—discreetly, of course—escort you out."

Joe placed a dollar in the agent's hand to go toward the change for coffee he'd asked for, and Miller stuffed it immediately into his pocket. He began to say something more when another guy dressed as a street person who was probably an agent motioned to him. Miller looked distracted, then with a dark scowl in Ripley's direction, he ambled toward the other man.

Between the real street people and the FBI disguised as the same, the place was abundant with odor and color. Joe had to give the agents credit. He couldn't tell them from the real deal, the baggy clothing allowing for plenty of room to hide weapons without telltale bulges. And the rain was certainly working in their favor. Had it been a nice day, it would have been a little difficult to pull off so many homeless men in one area at the same time.

"Looks like Polk spread the word," Joe murmured, steering Ripley toward the ticket window.

She stared at him. "At least we know Christine hasn't shown up yet. If she had, Miller wouldn't still be here."

Joe grimaced, not finding that bit of info the good news she obviously did.

He honestly didn't know what she hoped to accomplish here. But the fact that she wanted to do something only emphasized the differences between them. The longer he was around her, the more distanced he became from his own life. While that appealed to him on various levels and for various reasons in the beginning, now he felt more like a freshwater fish swimming in an unfamiliar sea. And he was starting to view Ripley as leading him straight into a school of sharks.

Somehow he'd never imagined when he eventually found someone to fall in love with that he would have to compromise. He'd always figured it would be the other way around. He had the successful company. He had the assets, the houses, the cars. He'd assumed the woman he'd want to spend the rest of his life with would have to compromise to be with him.

Instead, he was finding that everything he'd ever held dear was at risk. And he didn't know how he felt about that.

Yes, he did. He didn't feel very good about it at all. It was happening too fast. He felt like he was on an endless roller coaster that kept building up speed, going faster and faster, swinging through loops and careening around corners and shooting down slopes that left him gripping the bar in front of him for dear life. Never mind that he'd left his stomach somewhere in Memphis. All he wanted was for it to end so he could get off the sucker.

And the difference between him and Ripley was that she had her hands up in the air and was demanding that the ride go on and on....

THE LOCKER WAS to the right, second from the end and two rows from the floor. In the block of lockers closest to the side exit.

In the minute Joe had taken to give a dollar to Miller, Ripley had completely scoped out everything and everyone and was pretty sure she knew who was who in the crowded station. Miller she'd pegged immediately, even before he'd swooped down on them. He looked too healthy to be homeless. Too...hulky.

She stood behind a guy in line for tickets, trying to ignore the buzz of blood through her veins, fear and excitement a very heady mix.

Joe, on the other hand, looked ready to bolt for the door.

She squashed a smile. He looked so adorably sexy it was all she could do not to thread her fingers under that too small hat, then run them down the front of the only T-shirt she'd found that would fit him—a gift for Christmas from her parents that she wore as a night-shirt.

The man in front of her moved, and she stepped forward, scanning the schedule on the wall behind the attendant.

"I'm going to go get a newspaper," Joe grumbled beside her.

She smiled at him. "I'll be right here."

As she watched him walk away, she had to remind herself to tear her gaze away from his nicely shaped tush and give the station another once-over.

"God, I thought he'd never leave," a voice said from the other side of her. "No, don't look at me. Just casually turn to the attendant and ask for two tickets to Detroit."

Christine Bowman. Ripley didn't have to look to know it was her. It also didn't take much to figure out that she'd probably been in the bus station since before Ripley came in and that not one single agent had identified her.

Figured. Ripley had been having too much fun for something not to go wrong.

She did as Christine requested, then slid a glance toward the woman in question.

Christine had the audacity to smile at her. "I knew you wouldn't be able to resist coming here. Now, move casually, normally, toward the women's rest room. There, to the right."

Christine was decked out in full call-girl mode. Curly red wig. Bright red lipstick. Scarlet red dress that hugged her in all the right places. And a small black handbag that very obviously held the gun Ripley was far more familiar with than she wanted to be.

Oh, sure, Christine garnered the expected leers from every guy in the joint, agent or otherwise, but not a one of them seemed to put together that she was Christine Bowman.

Oh, boy.

"You know," Christine said, steering her toward the

ladies' room. "I didn't have a clue how I was going to get inside that locker what with all the G-men crowding the place." She nudged Ripley with her bag, the unmistakable metal jabbing into her side. "Then I saw you come in thinking you were going to fool me with that getup, and I knew I was saved."

Ripley smiled at Polk, trying to do a head tilt toward Christine, but Polk seemed too interested in checking out Christine's wares than in Ripley's subtle gestures.

The door to the ladies' room closed with an ominous click behind them. Christine checked inside the stalls, making sure they were empty, then threw the lock on the door, likely there to keep people from coming in while the room was cleaned.

"Strip."

Ripley blinked at her. "What?"

The handbag moved. "You heard me. Take off every last piece of clothing you've got on." She wrinkled her nose. "Except for your underwear. That, I can do without."

"Gee, thanks for small favors."

Ripley shrugged out of her coat, took off her hat, then her jeans and T-shirt, laying each over a nearby sink. The coat was an impulse buy last fall, an expensive designer name. But it was having to give up the shoes Joe had given her that annoyed her most.

"You know, you're never going to get out of here with those diamonds," she couldn't resist saying.

Christine's brows shot up as she kept her purse aimed with one hand and wiped off the loads of makeup she had caked on with the other. "So you know."

"Yes, I know. And I also know that a smart woman

would wait a day or two for things to calm down before trying to get them."

Christine slanted a look at her as she pulled off the wig. "That's what I said to myself two months ago. And look where that's gotten me." She blew out a long breath, carefully maneuvering the purse as she slipped out of her dress. She bent to pluck off one of her shoes.

Ripley shot forward, her intention to catch the woman off balance and grab her purse.

Christine instantly straightened and thrust the gun into Ripley's stomach. "I knew you'd do that." She pushed harder. "Get back."

Ripley did as she was ordered, hating that she'd left her gun at the apartment. *Don't worry*, she'd told herself, *there'll be enough firepower there to stop a horse.*

Only that horse had been wearing a slinky red dress and appeared to have a price tag stamped on her back.

A female agent would never have fallen for the getup.

"Put on the dress."

Ripley stared at her. "What?"

"You heard me." Christine slipped into the jeans, T-shirt and sneakers, all the while keeping the purse on Ripley. Ripley was only slightly mollified that the other woman couldn't do up the top button of the jeans.

Within moments, the two had completely swapped clothing and Ripley finished applying the lipstick Christine handed to her. She turned her head this way and that. She didn't look half bad as a redhead.

"Come on," Christine said, handing her the locker key then jabbing the purse into her side again.

"Would you stop? You're going to give me a bruise."

"You'll be lucky if a bruise is all you come away

with. Now get a move on." She unlocked the door and motioned for Ripley to precede her out. "I want you to head straight for the locker. Do not pass go, do not collect two hundred dollars. Got it?"

Ripley whipped her arm away. "You know, this probably all would have gone much smoother if you'd just paid me what was due."

"Move it."

And Ripley did. Straight to the locker. It wouldn't do any good to try to signal anyone. They would probably think she was looking for some business, given her new attire.

Except for Joe. Joe would certainly know that Christine wasn't her. Wouldn't he?

She glanced to find him leaning against the wall, pretending to read the business section of the newspaper, Agent Miller giving him an earful of what were undoubtedly threats. Neither one of them was looking in her direction.

Great. Just great.

She reached the lockers far more quickly than she would have thought, and her heart started beating double time in her chest. Things were definitely not looking good for her. She had little doubt of Christine's intentions once she had the diamonds in hand. Namely pull the trigger on the gun poking into her side and make a run for it. While Ripley didn't think the other woman's chances for escape were good, the chances Ripley would get out of the station without a little extra lead looked dim, indeed.

"Open it," Christine whispered, pretending an interest in the locker two up from the one in question. She put what looked like her lipstick in it, then added the coins that would release the key. Out of the corner of her eye, Ripley noticed Miller part from Joe then loom a little closer, probably wondering what the hell she was up to.

Ripley slid the key to the locker in and popped open the door. Only it was yawningly empty. Oh, boy.

"Give it to me!" Christine ordered harshly as half the homeless people in the station started closing in on them.

In a panic, Ripley scanned the faces of the under-cover agents, only to realize that the homeless men were real homeless men. Nelson's dearly beloved face was right in the middle of them. He winked at her. It was all she could do not to smile back.

"No problem," she said to Christine's request.

Ripley slammed the locker door open and right in Christine's face, reaching for the purse at the same time.

The homeless men, led by Nelson, swooped down on them from all sides. Nelson reached to help Ripley. The non-homeless agents had finally caught on and surrounded the others that surrounded them.

Only, unlike Nelson, they thought *she* was Christine.

"Wrong woman," Nelson shouted, grabbing an agent away from Ripley.

Ripley had a stranglehold on Christine's purse with one hand and reached up to pull off the wig with the other. The agents hesitated, obviously confused. Christine regained control of the gun and hit Ripley upside the head with it. Ripley smacked into the lockers, the din echoing through the station. In that one moment, she realized Christine might get away. Due to the agents' advance on them through the horde of home-less men, the path to the exit was left completely unblocked. Christine made a run for it. And with Ripley's sneakers, she just might make it.

A sound swirled up Ripley's throat, and she launched herself at the retreating figure, catching her around the knees and pulling her straight to the floor with a dull thud.

"Freeze!" someone finally yelled, and Ripley was half afraid it was she.

She turned to find it hadn't been her. Nelson, of all people, had shouted the command. The agents were all over her and Christine. They pulled Ripley to her feet, then confiscated Christine's purse and cuffed her on the spot.

Ripley gasped for air, trying not to notice the way her breasts threatened to spill out of the top of the dress or ponder the reason she was getting entirely too much of a breeze on her behind. Nelson gently moved her away from the ruckus.

She blinked at him. "How did you spot Christine?"

He grinned at her. "Simple. I know all the ho's that work the station, and she wasn't one of them."

Ripley laughed.

"Besides, she dressed more like the hundred-dollar variety, instead of the ten-dollar ones we usually get down here." He eyed her. "Red suits you."

"I'll remember that." Ripley turned to look for Joe, and her gaze fell instead on somebody else—a figure near the opposite door standing in partial shadow. The person stepped briefly into the light, her black vinyl rain slicker shimmering.

Nicole Bennett.

Ripley blinked as Nicole smiled.

Then she was gone.

# 14

JOE PATIENTLY applied antiseptic to Ripley's skinned knees. She sat at the dining table that dwarfed the room it was in. The apartment was small but neat, unassuming but filled with quality items, much like the woman herself. He swapped knees, and Ripley flinched. It was all Joe could do not to take a peek under the hem of the cotton shorts she'd put on after her shower to see what color underwear she had on.

He dragged the back of his hand across his forehead, thinking the place could stand some air-conditioning.

He slowly tuned in on Ripley's nonstop litany of the evening's events. The only time she'd hesitated in her speech was when he first hit each of her surface scrapes with the antiseptic.

"I about died when she told me to strip out of my clothes," she was saying, her brown eyes animated, her slender, sexy body radiating energy. "But you'll never guess who I saw after Christine's apprehension, standing calm as you please at the other end of the station."

Joe put the cap on the bottle and wadded up the cotton balls. "Who?" he asked without enthusiasm.

"Nicole Bennett."

That did prick his interest, but only because during two hours of grilling by Miller and his men, in which he and Ripley had had to repeat and repeat again everything that went down, Ripley had neglected to share that little piece of information.

Her smile was anything but repentant.

He sank back on his heels and rested his forearms on his thighs. "Let me get this straight. In the middle of everything going down, Nicole stood watching from the corner?"

"Uh-huh." Ripley got up, went to the refrigerator and took out two bottles of what looked like chocolate milk. She held one out to Joe. He took it even though he could have used a beer or something stronger right about then.

"So I guess we don't have to wonder where the diamonds went, then, do we?"

Unfortunately, Miller didn't seem all that convinced that Joe and Ripley weren't behind the missing gems. After all, they'd had the key in their possession until an hour before the grand opening of the locker.

Ripley led the way into the living room and he followed, sitting on the arm of an easy chair while she sprawled across the sofa. She took a long swallow of milk. "It was nothing but a wild-goose chase," she said half to herself. She turned her head to look at him. "The trip to Memphis, the pawnshop owner. When Nicole Bennett took that job at Christine Bowman's, she knew exactly what she was looking for. And it's my guess she had the diamonds five minutes after she got the key."

"But why the wild-goose chase?"

"Simple. She had to make sure Bowman was out of the picture or else she'd have her on her tail for however long it took to find her." A thoughtful expression wrinkled her lovely face. "She must have known the FBI had Christine under surveillance." She pulled at the label on the bottle. "I can't figure out how she got to the diamonds, though. Didn't Miller say they'd had the station staked out for the past two months?"

The more she talked, the more distant Joe became. He couldn't quite believe this was the same woman who'd had the muzzle of a gun pressed against her forehead, was forced to strip out of her clothes at gunpoint, then struggled with an armed woman all within the span of an hour.

She was looking at him. He sighed. "It's my guess that once Bowman picked up stakes here and they followed you to Memphis, they lightened manpower at the bus station. It wouldn't have taken much for her to have arranged for some sort of distraction, taken the diamonds, then returned to Memphis."

She sat up. "That's right. Nicole didn't sell the box to the pawnshop owner until a day later."

Joe stared at the bottle in his hand, started to take a drink, then grimaced. He put it on the coffee table, untouched.

Now that the mystery was solved, Ripley seemed to have run out of gas. Unfortunately, Joe had run out of gas somewhere between Memphis and St. Louis. And with the threat hanging over their heads gone...well, he felt more at odds than ever.

"Joe?" Ripley said quietly.

When he looked at her, the frown she wore told him it wasn't the first time she had said his name.

"Is everything all right?" she asked.

"Everything's fine," he said. But the moment the words were out of his mouth, he recognized the lie for what it was. He pushed from the chair arm and paced a short way away, running his hand over his hair. "Actually, no. Everything's not fine."

While she was in the shower, he'd used a towel to dry his hair then stripped out of the T-shirt she'd loaned him. He was in his trusty old white shirt, tie and slacks. Only, when he looked down, he barely recognized himself. What did it mean when a guy didn't feel comfortable in his own clothes?

He turned toward Ripley, his gaze settling on her unforgettable face. A need so intense, so overwhelming, gripped his stomach, making him want to stride across the room, sweep her up from the couch and carry her off to the bed that lay behind the door just a few feet away.

"I've got to go."

Joe heard the words. Saw Ripley wince from the impact. But for the life of him he didn't think he'd said them. But there they lay. Hovering between them like a bird neither of them wanted to catch.

Ripley was the first to glance away. She slowly put her bottle on the table next to his, the pain on her face ripping him in two.

"I see," she said quietly.

Joe strode to collect his suitcase from the dining room and placed it next to the door. "Do you? Because I sure as hell don't see much right now."

She got up from the couch. He nearly held his hand out and shouted, "don't," for fear that he would never get out of that door if she moved within touching range.

Instead he stood pole straight, his throat tight and raw as she stepped haltingly in front of him. She looked about to hug him, withdrew, then went ahead and threw her slender arms around his neck anyway, resting her cheek on his shoulder and facing away from him. Joe closed his eyes and swallowed hard. Her breasts pressed against his chest, making his heart kick up, while her hips nestled snugly against his, making other parts of his anatomy kick up. Parts he didn't want to acknowledge. Hadn't they already gotten him into enough trouble?

"Thank you," Ripley whispered in his ear, pressing her soft lips against his neck.

Joe groaned, unable to hold back. His arms curved around her, tugging her closer, every part of him reveling in the feeling of her nearness. He'd never experienced emotions so pure, so out of control, before. And, simply, they scared him more than the gun Christine had wielded.

Looking back, he realized he'd always had a certain vision of his life and how it would turn out. And everything that had happened over the past few days was so far outside that as to emerge surreal. He had the company he'd built up with his own two hands, his family in Minneapolis—everything that was familiar and safe and his.

"Where will you go?" she asked, her arms holding him even tighter.

"To Memphis, I guess. I'll get my car." And attempt to put his life back into some sort of order. Maybe contact the reps at Shoes Plus and try to make amends. Or maybe he'd drive straight to Minneapolis. Being home might help snap him out of his zombielike state.

He heard her breath catch. "You, um, could stay here."

Joe nearly groaned at her whispered words.

"You know, for tonight. You could leave in the morning."

Of course. What had he expected? That she was asking him to stay for good? And what if she had? Would he have stayed? Joe didn't know. And that scared him more than everything else combined.

He somehow found the courage to set her away from him. "I can't." He'd rent a car and drive to Memphis if he had to. He didn't care. He knew he had to get out of here...now, before he made an even bigger fool of himself.

Ripley's brown eyes were soft and watery.

He turned toward the door.

"Joe?"

He braced himself but refused to face her.

"Will I see you again?"

He silently cursed. "It depends."

"On what?"

"On whether business brings me through St. Louis or not."

He hated saying the words, but for the life of him he couldn't come up with anything else.

He opened the door and walked out.

RIPLEY STOOD staring at the closed door for so long her eyes hurt. She couldn't quite bring herself to believe he'd just walked out like that. Every bit of adrenaline that had been roaring through her system from the night's events had stopped midstream. What had just happened? Was it something she said? Something she did?

Forcing her legs into action, she hurried toward the window, peering out much as she had earlier. But instead of trying to spot the FBI surveillance vehicles, she sought Joe's familiar silhouette. There. There he was. He'd crossed the street and was walking, head down in the rain, toward downtown. She opened her mouth to call to him through the open window, but that's how her mouth stayed. Open. Silent.

What could she say to him? "Come back?" She'd already asked him to stay, and he'd turned her down cold.

He turned the corner and walked out of sight.

Ripley felt as if her heart had dropped to the floor at her feet and if she wasn't careful she'd step on it. Just as surely as Joe had stomped all over it just now.

Was she a little slow on the uptake or what? She'd been so consumed with the Bowman case she hadn't even stopped to examine what was happening between her and Joe. She absently ran a hand down her face, surprised to find tears clinging to her cheeks. She remembered him trying to talk to her earlier, when they had returned to her apartment. Recalled the somber expression he'd been wearing since before then. What had he been thinking? What had he wanted to say?

She didn't know what was worse. That she didn't know. Or that she would never know.

She sank to the floor, her back against the wall beneath the window, mindless of the spray of rain the wind blew in every now and again.

One thing she did know was that for the first time in her life, she'd fallen in love with a guy. Hard. Kissing asphalt hard. She'd said and done things to and with him she'd never done with another man. She waited to feel ashamed. Instead she felt a pain the size of Missouri spread slowly across her chest.

Had she really been that shortsighted not to notice until it was too late the signs that she loved Joe? Or had she simply been too afraid? Had she poured so much of her courage into her career that she didn't have any left over for him? For love?

Some private investigator she was. Oh, sure, she'd done a bang-up job on the Bowman case. But when it came to her personal life, she couldn't tell the difference between great sex and full-blown love. And she'd just let the best thing in her life walk right out that door.

She remembered what Polk had once told her. That he hadn't met a woman who lived up to his idea of one. She questioned that wisdom. In fact, the more she considered it, the more she thought it was just so much bull. It wasn't that the idea was better. It was that he'd probably spent so damn much time on his job, he hadn't paid attention to what was standing right in front of him.

And here she'd gone and made the same stinking mistake.

TWO MONTHS LATER, Ripley leaned back in her scratched and dented office chair and lifted her feet to prop them on the desktop. The spring in the chair threatened to dump her onto the floor. Grabbing the edge of the desk, she righted herself.

To add insult to injury, her mentor and coconspirator Nelson Polk was watching her from the other side of the rented office space, his bushy gray eyebrows hovering over his amusement-filled eyes. "Careful there. You don't have disability insurance yet. You just opened this place. Be a shame to have to close it so quickly."

Ripley settled for sitting back carefully and folding her hands over her stomach. So she was in jeans and a sweatshirt rather than a wrinkled old suit and overcoat, but what mattered was how she felt. And she felt like a private investigator through and through. From the green and gold lettering she'd splurged on for the front window announcing that Ripley Logan, Private Investigator, had arrived, to the newspaper clippings she had framed and hung on the wall to her left, her dreams had come true.

Her mood dampened considerably.

Well, almost. She hadn't known she wanted that other dream, so it didn't really count, did it? A grainy picture from the St. Louis *Times and Tribune* caught her eye. It was a shot of her and Joe coming out of the bus station, Joe holding a newspaper over her head as rain pounded down on them. It was her complete rapture as she looked at him that made her heart skip a beat.

Okay, so maybe things hadn't completely turned out the way she would have liked them to. She got the job but lost the man. But at least she'd had him for a little while, which was more than a woman like her should expect. Right?

She made a face. What a crock that one was. That's exactly what the old Ripley would have thought. The Ripley who whined about paper cuts and filing and the general miserable state of her life. A woman who hadn't gotten a lot out of her love life because she hadn't expected much from it. Now... Well, now she demanded more. In her professional life, she'd lived by two philosophies—put everything on the line and let the dice fall where they may. Thankfully, they'd given her a winning combination until now. Unfortunately, she wasn't so brave when it came to her personal life.

But she planned to change that, as well.

She cleared her throat, watching Nelson fix a filing cabinet on the other side of the large room. He slid the drawer in and out, then picked up the screwdriver again.

After Joe left, she leaned on Polk more than she ever had before. Thankfully she'd never again seen him in the state he'd been in the day she'd sobered him up and he'd told her where the locker was. In fact, she was beginning to suspect he'd put the drink away for good a few weeks ago.

She couldn't be completely sure what had caused him to drink himself into a stupor that afternoon, but she guessed the young man she'd seen him with the other day had something to do with it. His son? She suspected so. He only had one, and she knew from what he'd told her during one of their many conversations that he hadn't seen the boy since he was three years old. His showing up after so many years would be enough to send anyone diving into a liquor bottle. It also appeared to be a catalyst for him to stop.

Of course, she didn't think the Bowman case had hurt any, either. At the bus station when he'd helped apprehend Christine, she didn't think she'd seen Polk so alive. So alert. And then changes began occurring little by little in his everyday life. Gone were the tattered, smelly clothes, replaced with clean new clothes she'd helped him shop for with the money he'd had stashed in a savings account but hadn't accessed for years. He'd gotten a haircut, shaved every day and had moved into a boardinghouse not far from the office. She'd thought she'd be doing him a favor when she hired him to work part-time at the office. The truth was, he was doing her a favor. She'd had no idea how to handle the avalanche of clients that had come knocking after the press coverage of her involvement in the Bowman case. She was turning people away.

"Nelson?"

"Hmm?" He looked up from the filing cabinet.

"Do you ever wonder if you let the business run you instead of you running the business?"

He squinted at her. It was hard to believe that a short time ago he'd been little more than a park drunk who could play a great game of chess and had tons of stories about his P.I. adventures. "What's that again?"

Ripley fingered a file in front of her. It was bursting at the seams. "I just wonder if you ever regret not giving as much attention to your personal life as you gave to being a P.I."

"Every day I open my eyes."

She didn't say anything. She nodded, then absently opened the file in front of her. A picture of Joe Pruitt virtually jumped out at her.

Okay, so maybe she hadn't completely let him go. While physically he was no longer a part of her life, she'd made him a part of it by scrounging every last bit of information she could on the college basketball player turned entrepreneur. She cringed as she remembered introducing him as a shoe salesman. From what she had gathered from news pieces on his success, that would be akin to his calling her a bike messenger.

She turned over the promotional photo she'd obtained by contacting his PR department and looked through the various news clippings she'd compiled. From posing with sports stars even she recognized to hosting charitable events, he was a man unfamiliar to her. Sure, he looked the same, but the Joe she knew couldn't have been more different from this man.

She turned over a press clipping and stopped to stare at another one. It was the last one she'd collected before calling a halt to her efforts a month ago. From the society pages of the Minneapolis *Star*, it showed Joe with a pretty brunette at some event or another. A formal one that spotlighted Joe in a tux and the woman in something sexy and shimmering. The columnist predicted future wedding bells for the couple, Joe a self-made man, the woman from a successful, wealthy Minneapolis family.

Ripley predicted the end of her mooning over a man she'd let slip right through her fingers. At least she hoped it would end.

"Go after him."

She blinked several times then stared at Polk. He'd finished with the filing cabinet and was putting a fern on top of it. "What?"

He grinned, and she knew he wouldn't repeat himself. They both knew very well that she'd heard him.

"Mail call." Nelson opened the door and collected the morning delivery from the mailman.

Ripley sat up and accepted the small pile of mail from him. She'd only been in the office a month, so she wasn't expecting much. Water bill, gas bill, telephone bill, a letter from the Grand Bahamas...

She turned the envelope over, then over again. Nothing to indicate who the envelope was from. Just a postmark. She checked the address. Sure enough, it was directed to Ripley Logan, Private Investigator.

"What is it?" Nelson asked.

She shrugged. "I don't know."

She opened the middle desk drawer, starting when the drawer nearly fell out of its track and into her lap. She freed her letter opener and slid a neat opening into the envelope. Blowing between the flaps, she turned the envelope upside down and watched as a yellow slip of paper the length and width of the envelope drifted down on the air, then landed smack dab in the middle of her desk.

She leaned closer for a better look. It was a cashier's check...made out for ten thousand dollars.

Ripley nearly swallowed her tongue.

"Well, if that isn't a nice chunk of change," Polk said, lifting a coffee cup she hoped was filled with only coffee or else she might be tempted to down the contents.

"Um, yeah."

The question was, where had it come from? She was

almost afraid to touch the check. Merely looking at it, she felt like she was breaking the law. She slid the letter opener under the right-hand corner and gave a flick. The check flipped to lie face down. The initials NB were written right in the middle, along with a smiley face.

Nicole Bennett.

"Oh, boy. She did get the diamonds."

"What? Who?"

Ripley stared unseeingly at Nelson, then slowly brought him into focus. "Nicole Bennett."

Polk grinned and took one of the mismatched visitors' chairs in front of the desk. He didn't have one problem with his chair when he propped his feet on the corner of the desk. "Smart cookie, that one."

Ripley blinked at him. Smart cookie had to be the understatement of the year. The brunette had played them all like a fine-tuned guitar, making it appear that she had unwittingly stolen from another thief, leading them on a wild-goose chase to Memphis to get them out of St. Louis, then setting up the original thief with the skill of a professional. Unfortunately, the dead pawnshop owner probably didn't find the whole fiasco amusing. But from what Ripley had read about the initial robbery in New York, the Memphis man hadn't been Christine Bowman's first or only victim. Two security guards had been shot and killed in the heist, a third paralyzed for life.

Ripley sat back and stared at Polk. "What should I do with it?"

"What do you mean what should you do with it? You should cash it, of course." He grinned at her, showing the result of recent dental work. "And give me a raise."

"But it's blood money."

"Blood you had no hand in spilling, and neither did Nicole Bennett." He sighed and glanced at the wall where an FBI artist had drawn three different composites of the mystery woman in question. "All thieves should be as savvy as her. Commit victimless crimes."

Ripley sat back and shook her head, still staring at the check. "There's no way I can cash this."

"Take the money, Ripley. You earned it."

Her breath caught in her throat, her gaze flying to the man who'd spoken from the doorway.

Neither she nor Nelson had heard him come in. Checks of this amount probably had a tendency to do that to people.

"How are you doing, Joe?" Nelson got up, walked over to the stud in athletic shoes and shook his hand.

Joe's gaze strayed from Ripley's face to consider the older man. He blinked several times. "Nelson Polk?"

"One and the same." They dropped hands then Polk glanced at her. "I think I'll just go...run that errand now."

"Errand...right," Ripley repeated dumbly.

The door closed behind him. Peripherally she saw him pause in front of the glass window, indicating she should proceed. Do something. Then he threw his hands in the air and continued down the sidewalk.

"Um, hi," Ripley said.

Forget chair springs. Joe's grin nearly knocked her chair legs right out from under her. He sauntered to the front of the desk. "You should take it, you know. The money."

She finally forced herself to blink.

"After all, you never did get paid the rest of your fee."

"Yes, but the total would never come to this much."

"Then consider it a bonus."

A thought occurred to her. "You...you wouldn't happen to be behind this, would you?"

"Me?" He seemed to understand what she was asking. "Oh, God, no. But I'm thinking that maybe I should have done something."

So Nicole really had sent her the check. And Joe Pruitt was really standing in front of her looking more delicious than ever.

Her gaze flicked over him. Gone were the white shirt, tie and slacks. In their place were a pair of gray sweatpants and a dark blue T-shirt that brought out the color of his eyes. In fact...

"You didn't run all the way from Minneapolis, did you?" she asked.

His chuckle did funny things to her stomach. "No." He looked around the office, then his gaze stopped on something on her desk. After a long moment, Ripley realized it was the file she'd compiled on him.

She smacked it closed and shoved it into a desk drawer.

"Just some..." She wasn't sure what to say. They both knew what the file was.

His grin widened. "Actually, I'm living in St. Louis now."

Forget the chair legs, Ripley nearly fell clean off the chair. "What? When? How long?"

He motioned toward her drawer. "Had you kept up on your information, you would have known it was a month ago." He cleared his throat. "About the same time you opened the doors here."

He knew she'd opened her own agency? He'd moved to St. Louis? And he hadn't contacted her?

"You're confused."

"Um, yes, I am. How—why haven't you tried to contact me before now?"

The grin disappeared, and that serious expression she'd learned to fear came back. "I could ask why you didn't pursue me to Minneapolis."

"If you'd asked, I'd have told you. Because I'm a coward."

His eyes practically devoured her, as if she'd said the one thing he'd needed to hear most.

He crossed his arms over his wide chest, drawing attention to the sweat stains. He looked as if he'd been jogging. The idea that he'd been running by her office for the past month without her knowing it made her feel suddenly dizzy.

"Actually, there's a specific reason I stopped by now."

She searched his eyes. "Oh?"

He nodded. "You see, I want to hire you to help me find someone."

"I see." She tried to hide her disappointment. She'd thought he'd stopped by to see her, and instead he was in need of her services. She shakily pulled her yellow legal pad in front of her and grabbed a pen. "Who?"

"Me."

She slowly looked up.

He shifted from one foot to the other. "You see, there's this guy I used to know." His voice dropped to a low murmur that skated over her skin. "This guy...we'll call him Joe. And Joe, well, he used to be pretty satisfied with his life. He'd accomplished more than either of his parents had ever expected of him, built a successful business from the ground up, and generally enjoyed what he had—which, from a material standpoint, was a lot." His gaze swept everywhere but over her as he spoke. "Then one day he met this woman." He finally looked at her. "We'll call her Ripley."

Her heart dipped to her feet then bounded up again.

"And she...well, she turned everything upside down. She made down look up. She made white look black. And she made Joe realize that he'd never really been happy with what he had. She showed him that he'd merely settled. Taken the road well traveled.

"This woman, Ripley, well, one day, after some of the most incredible sex Joe had ever had, she asked him what he would like to do if he could chose to do anything in the world. You see, he didn't answer her. Because to do so would be to open a door that could reveal something he didn't want to know.

"Then he left her, Joe did, even though it ripped his heart out to do so. He thought that if he just went home, got back into the same routine, everything would be fine. He wouldn't have to think about that question, the mind-blowing sex or the woman who had given him both.

"The only problem is, there was no going back. No matter how hard Joe tried, he couldn't forget the incredible woman who had swept into his life, this Ripley. It took him a month to figure out that he probably never would. He's got a hard head, this Joe."

Ripley stared at him, spellbound.

"So Joe named his secretary CEO of his company headquarters in Minneapolis and not only answered that question Ripley had once asked him, he pursued it. He's now in St. Louis and is first assistant basketball coach at Washington University in St. Louis."

Ripley didn't quite know what to say. So she said nothing.

"And now Joe would like to know how the woman, this Ripley, feels about everything he's just told her."

How did she feel? Ripley searched her heart and her mind. She felt like the most important woman on earth for having done something to deserve the man in front of her. Like she must not have totally screwed up for him to have come back to her.

She catapulted from the chair and practically dove into his arms, catching his head in her hands and planting a kiss on him that had them both panting for air. He tasted like fresh air, sweat and the man she loved.

"So?" he asked, running his thumb over her bottom lip. "What do you say? I can promise you you'll never want for another pair of shoes again in your life."

She scanned his handsome face from forehead to chin, wondering if she'd ever missed anyone so much. "Joe, my feet are yours to do with what you will. But try putting a wedding ring on my toe instead of my finger and you're in big trouble."

"I have other things in mind for your toes," he said with a sexy grin. "And, just this once, let me get in the last word."

Just before he silenced her with one of his breath-stealing kisses, she murmured, "Never."

\* \* \* \* \*

*Look for Nicole Bennett's story in the special*
**BAD GIRLS**
*trilogy in early 2003!*

COOPER'S CORNER

**In April 2002 you are invited to three wonderful
weddings in a very special town...**

# A Wedding at
# Cooper's Corner

**USA Today bestselling author**

# Kristine Rolofson
# Muriel Jensen
# Bobby Hutchinson

Ailing Warren Cooper has asked private investigator
David Solomon to deliver three precious envelopes to each
of his grandchildren. Inside each is something that will bring
surprise, betrayal...and unexpected romance!

And look for the exciting launch of *Cooper's Corner*,
a NEW 12-book continuity from Harlequin—
launching in August 2002.

# HARLEQUIN®
*Makes any time special*®

Visit us at www.eHarlequin.com

PHWCC

# magazine

♥——————————————————— **quizzes**

Is he the one? What kind of lover are you? Visit the Quizzes area to find out!

♥——————————————————— **recipes for romance**

Get scrumptious meal ideas with our Recipes for Romance.

♥——————————————————— **romantic movies**

Peek at the Romantic Movies area to find Top 10 Flicks about First Love, ten Supersexy Movies, and more.

♥——————————————————— **royal romance**

Get the latest scoop on your favorite royals in Royal Romance.

♥——————————————————— **games**

Check out the Games pages to find a ton of interactive romantic fun!

♥——————————————————— **romantic travel**

In need of a romantic rendezvous? Visit the Romantic Travel section for articles and guides.

♥——————————————————— **lovescopes**

Are you two compatible? Click your way to the Lovescopes area to find out now!

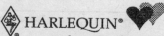

**makes any time special—online...**

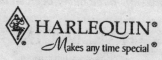

**HARLEQUIN**

*Temptation*

THE WRONG BED

What happens when a girl finds herself in the
*wrong* bed...with the *right* guy?

*Find out in:*

**#866 NAUGHTY BY NATURE by Jule McBride**
February 2002

**#870 SOMETHING WILD by Toni Blake**
March 2002

**#874 CARRIED AWAY by Donna Kauffman**
April 2002

**#878 HER PERFECT STRANGER by Jill Shalvis**
May 2002

**#882 BARELY MISTAKEN by Jennifer LaBrecque**
June 2002

**#886 TWO TO TANGLE by Leslie Kelly**
July 2002

*Midnight mix-ups have never been so much fun!*

**HARLEQUIN®**
*Makes any time special®*

HTNBN2